THE TRUTH ABOUT US

ALY MARTINEZ

The Truth About Us
Copyright © 2018 Aly Martinez

ISBN: 978-1727156768
ISBN-10: 1727156765

The Truth About Us is a work of fiction. All names, characters, places, and occurrences are the product of the author's imagination. Any resemblance to any persons, living or dead, events, or locations is purely coincidental.

Cover Designer: Hang Le
Photography: Wander Aguiar
Editing: Mickey Reed
Proofreader: Julie Deaton
Formatting: Stacey Blake

THE
TRUTH
ABOUT
US

PROLOGUE

Penn

One minute before I lost her...

A hotel room. That's where I was leaving Cora.

A fucking hotel room with shitty commercial carpet that made my skin crawl. Sure, it was a nice place with full-time security, and I'd made sure we were on the top floor, but the idea of leaving her in a goddamn hotel room had turned my blood to sludge.

It was the only way. I needed her out of that apartment building for a night—and then forever.

I stared at the side of her face, her lips parted in slumber, and committed each and every curve to memory. Her smooth skin, her long lashes, even that tiny mole below her lip.

All of it was mine.

She was mine.

And in order to save her, I had to let her go.

I could give her the money. I had enough. But as long as the Guerrero brothers were still sharing the Earth's oxygen, she'd never be free.

They would find her, manipulate her, punish her, and I had not one doubt they would ultimately kill her.

And while I was out exacting revenge for a woman I'd loved but hadn't been able to save, the cycle would repeat itself.

We all had choices in life.

I could have stayed.

I could have kept Cora.

I could have taken her and River away, put them up in a fancy house with private security, but they'd always be looking over their shoulders.

That wasn't freedom. That was moving them from one prison to another.

And it would have solved *nothing*.

Thomas Lyons, the very man who had ordered my wife's death, was a part of Cora's world. From what I could tell, she was helping his wife, Catalina, and his daughter, Isabel, hide from him. One day, he'd find out and come after Cora too.

My worlds had officially bled together, and Thomas, the city's beloved district attorney with the perfect record, was the source of the wound.

So, at the end of the day, I had no choice at all.

The only thing I could do was keep the blood off *her* hands.

Even if that meant stabbing myself in the heart and disappearing from her life altogether.

She'd be okay.

She'd recover, move on, make a life of her own.

I wouldn't. Not ever. But I'd at least be able to rest at

night, knowing she was safely sleeping under the stars.

One in. One out.

I closed my eyes, pressed a kiss to her forehead, and then filled my lungs with all things Cora Guerrero.

Her laugh.

Her smile.

Her kind heart.

Her selfless nature.

The way she loved.

The way she gave.

The way she'd brought me back to life.

"Truth," I whispered against her temple. "I love you."

She didn't budge as I crawled out of bed.

She didn't budge as I waged war with my body in order to force my legs to carry me away from her.

And she didn't budge when the flames of hell finally devoured me as I stepped into the hall and silently pulled the door shut.

"You ready?" Drew asked.

I'd texted him the minute her breathing had evened out. Though I'd probably kept him waiting longer than I should have.

I ground my teeth to cover the emotion. "Swear to me you will take care of her."

His fierce, brown eyes locked on my blues. "Swear to *me* you will kill those motherfuckers and then come back alive."

I extended a hand in his direction. "Done."

He grinned, clapping his hand with mine. "Then you have my word."

We started toward the elevator on the same foot, my entire body screaming as I left her there. I had known that it was wrong the minute I'd decided to do it. But my back was against the wall.

"I don't feel right about letting her think I was stealing the money," I told him.

His hand snaked out, catching my bicep, stopping me mid-step. "You *have* to do that. Do you hear me? You are not another man she needs to spend thirteen years pining after. You get her money, put it in your toolbox, and make it look like Dante and Marcos just happened to show up as you were taking off with it."

"She won't believe that, Drew. She's gonna see straight through this."

He stepped in front of me, his eyebrows furrowed, and stabbed a finger in my chest. "Then *make* her believe it. I'll help on my end, planting that seed as best I can if she doesn't jump to the conclusion on her own, but I'm not about to spend the next six months consoling a woman who thinks her poor, sweet boyfriend was torched while trying to protect her honor. She will not recover from that, Penn. She will spend the rest of her life blaming herself for getting an innocent man killed and you know it." He poked at my chest, punctuating every sentence. "Be the bad guy. Take the fall. Let her get pissed. Break her fucking heart. And help her let you go."

The problem was I didn't *want* her to let me go. But I couldn't take her with me. For a myriad of reasons, I needed to put as much distance as I could between Cora Guerrero and Thomas Lyons. The biggest being that, if and when my true identity was linked to Penn Walker, she would be either his next target or a suspect in his murder. So far, I—Shane Pennington—was free and clear. Those hundreds of thousands of dollars I'd spent buying a new identity had paid off. For her sake, I needed to keep it that way. But I couldn't leave until I was positive she was as far removed from this entire clusterfuck as I could get her.

Or, as it turned out, as far away as *Drew* could get her.

I clipped him with my shoulder as I marched past him to the elevator and then jabbed the button.

Drew wasn't done with his lecture yet. "I swear to God, if you try to stray from the plan, I will find you and kill you myself. You are not the good guy anymore. She is going to be a wreck when you die either way, but hating you will be easier. She knows how to deal with shit situations, Penn."

"But that's just it. That's all she's ever been given. Shit, shit, and more shit. And, now, I'm adding to that shit."

Suddenly, he was in my face. "I'm not going to be there to save your ass if this goes south. You get the money, put it in your toolbox, and then you leave it on the seat of the truck. The cops shouldn't search it since it's in my name, but if they do, I'll produce the bank records where Shane Pennington gave his best friend who just got out of jail a loan. Cora won't have to know about that. And if she finds out, I'll lie and say my money burned up in the fire. We have thought out every possible angle to put her at the least amount of risk. Do not go off script now. This is not one of those times you can play loose. You gotta stop obsessing over the shit you can't change and focus on actually surviving this bullshit. Taking down not one, but two Guerreros is not going to be easy."

My bones ached like they were being snapped in two. "I promise you it'll be easier than leaving her."

"Probably. But I'd prefer to hear you crying about a woman any day of the week over putting you in the ground. So I'll repeat: *Focus.* There is plenty of time to cry into your cornflakes later."

I shot him a scowl, but the levity did start to ease the pressure in my chest. "Right."

"Now. Are you sure I can't go with you? I've been jonesing to throw a match at Dante's feet for quite a while."

The elevator dinged. "No. You stay with her. If something really happens to me…you—"

He gave my shoulder a squeeze. "I got it. One million, one hundred, a fuck-ton of other numbers, and ninety-nine cents."

Holding his gaze, I swallowed hard, a mountain of unspoken words dividing us. Drew had been my best friend for seventeen years. He'd become my family when I'd married his sister. And when we'd lost her, he'd become my partner in a quest for vengeance.

And, right then, there was a very solid chance that I wasn't leaving just Cora that night.

"Drew… I—"

"Don't you dare. You get your ass out of here. Do your thing. We'll have a beer and catch up in a few months when this is all said and done, yeah?"

"Yeah," I whispered.

"Now, go. Get out of here before you get all emotional and your dick falls off. You just recently got it back. I'd hate to see you lose it again."

I barked a laugh. Goddamn it. He was a good man.

With one last tip of my chin, I walked into the elevator and stared at the floor as the doors slid shut.

On the way down to the first floor, a lot of things happened:

My mind cleared.

My resolve clicked back into place.

And that all-too-familiar numbness washed back over me.

Penn Walker climbed onto the elevator that night, but when the doors opened at the bottom, Shane Pennington walked out focused, determined, and fueled by more pain than ever before.

The problem was, only a few hours later, I realized they were both irrevocably in love with Cora Guerrero.

CHAPTER ONE

Cora

Four years earlier...

"Chrissy!" I yelled, banging on the door to her apartment. I glanced over at Angela, who was standing in the walkway, chewing on her bottom lip. "You did the right thing."

"We'll see," she muttered, turning her nerves onto her fingernails.

I started searching through my key ring. "Ang, listen to me. If she brings a john here, it puts us all at risk. At risk of the cops finding out. Or Dante or Marcos. Or, hell, even Manuel. I don't know about you, but I'm not willing to hang my ass out on a limb for Chrissy to make a couple bucks on the side."

"No. I know. It's just I feel bad. She's my girl, ya know?"

I shoved the key into the lock. "If she was really your girl, she wouldn't have put you in this position to begin with." I didn't have a chance to turn the key before the door swung open.

Chrissy appeared in the entryway wearing a black

nighty. Her thick, dyed dark hair was disheveled, and her lipstick lined the outer rim of her mouth. "Would you stop filling her head with bullshit?" She leaned out to glare at Angela. "I'm gonna fucking sew your mouth shut."

Angela's back straightened and her eyes flashed wide before she slunk into her apartment.

"Do you have to be such a bitch all the time?" I asked.

Chrissy grinned, all toothy and yellow. "I could ask you the same question."

I scoffed. "I'm the bitch? You bring a john here, putting every woman in this building in danger, yet I'm the bitch? Jesus, Chrissy. Pull your damn head out of your ass for a minute and think about someone other than yourself."

She rolled her eyes, propping her shoulder against the jamb, grinning like I'd told a joke. "I don't know what you're talking about. There's no man here." She swung her arm out, inviting me in. "See for yourself."

With less than zero interest in trudging through her trashy apartment in search of an even trashier man, I snapped, "Get him out. Now."

"There's nobody here." She pouted her lips and drew an invisible X over her heart.

Then a woman's voice I didn't recognize came from behind me. "Uhhhh, because he's right there."

Spinning around, I caught sight of a half-naked man sprinting out of the parking lot. Luckily for me, it was the lower half that was covered. Though, after having witnessed his fur-covered stomach bouncing in the breeze, I wasn't sure *luck* was the right term.

"Oh, would you look at that," Chrissy breathed in mock

disbelief. "You know, you should really have a chat with Angela. I saw her sneaking a guy in earlier, but I didn't want to rat her out. You know being that we're *girls* and all."

I swung my burning retinas back on her. "Are you fucking kidding me, Chris? You of all people know better than—"

"Who the hell is she?" She jerked her chin toward the parking lot.

On reflex, I looked over my shoulder and found a tall, leggy brunette standing just inside the breezeway. She was wearing pink shorts that hugged her thin figure and a white silk camisole that didn't show nearly enough cleavage for this profession but entirely too much for her to be a Jehovah's Witness come to save my soul.

"Can I help you?" I asked just before Chrissy's door slammed shut. I let out a groan, vowing to deal with her later. Though, short of calling in a Guerrero—which, no fucking way—there wasn't much more I could do.

The woman smiled, revealing what had to be a small fortune in childhood orthodontics and a diet of clouds.

She pointed a manicured nail at Chrissy's door. "She seems nice."

"A real prize," I replied, giving her another once-over. "What can I do for you today?"

"Oh, right." She walked over, forcing me to crane my head back to see her.

I was short, but she had to have been at least six feet tall in those strappy, nude wedges.

Warm, brown eyes stared down at me as she asked, "I'm looking for Dante Guerrero."

3

I curled my lip. "Well, that's unfortunate. He doesn't live here."

She cocked her head to the side like a confused puppy. "But he owns the building, right?"

"That he does." I opened my arms, waving them around, doing my best impression of a *The Price Is Right* model. "But, somehow, he manages to resist the urge to make this luxurious palace his primary residence."

"Do you, um…know how I could get in touch with him? He told me to meet him here, but I didn't get his number."

The hairs on the back of my neck stood on end as panic flooded in my system. "Shit! He's coming here? *Today?*"

"Um… Well, not today, *today*. He just gave me this address and told me to come over whenever I…um… had the chance. So here I am."

I blew out a loud breath, patting my chest as if I could manually slow my racing heart. "Jesus. Don't scare me like that."

"Sorry," she whispered sheepishly.

Up close, she was even prettier. She was older than I was, maybe thirty, but she had good skin and a nice, subtle hand with makeup. She wasn't the kind of beautiful that would grace the pages of a magazine, but she was definitely pretty enough to think that maybe she could. The thought made me cringe.

"Can I ask what kind of business you have with Dante?"

"Oh, um…." Her eyes lit. "I answered an ad online—"

"For a model?" I finished for her.

"Yes! Exactly."

4

I sighed. How the hell he managed to find this many desperate women was beyond me. And one that looked like this? Forget it.

"Listen. You seem nice. So I'm gonna let you in on a little secret." I leaned in close and lowered my voice to a whisper. "It's not what you think. It's a…scam. Go home and forget about it. You do not want any part of this."

I started to turn away, but she caught my arm.

"I got nowhere to go. I used the last of my money I had to catch a cab over here today. Look, I know what happens here. I got clients of my own. Rich ones. I'm just shifting teams. That's all."

Jerking my arm away, I stared at her in mock awe. "You're from another stable?"

She nodded repeatedly.

"You got johns of your own?"

She nodded again.

"And Dante gave you this address?"

More with the bobble head impression.

I eyed her warily, searching for the truth in her big doe eyes.

There was none to be found.

"You're so full of shit. We don't run that kind of business here. Get the fuck off my property."

"Okay, fine! I'm not from another…stable. But I've got experience."

I rolled my eyes, giving her my back as I started toward the stairs. My phone started ringing, and after I'd dug it from my back pocket, Manuel's number showed on the screen.

"No. No. No. Wait!" she cried.

But I ignored her, knowing better than to let his call go to voicemail. "Hello."

"She's fucking pregnant!" he boomed.

Wannabe-supermodel Heidi Klum followed me up, whispering pleas with every step.

"Who?" I asked Manuel, stopping on the second floor to snap my finger and point to the parking lot. Then I mouthed a stern, "*Get out.*"

She lifted her hands in prayer. "Please. Just hear me out."

Manuel kept ranting in my ear. "I don't fucking know. Whatever the hell bitch you took to the doctor this morning."

Shit. Lucy.

"Turn her out, Cora."

"No, wait," I breathed.

The woman's face lit.

"Not you!" I hissed at her.

Manuel continued. "I fucking warned you. She's gone. Tonight. And if I have to come over there and do it myself, I swear to God, I'm taking River home with me."

My head spun as all the blood drained from my face. I reached out, grabbing the railing to balance myself. "No. No. I'll take care of it. I swear. Lucy's gone. Right now."

"Good. Now, thanks to your stupidity, I'm down a girl. So I don't give a fuck if you have to hit the street yourself to make it happen, but I want double the haul tonight. You fucking owe me that."

I didn't know how he could possibly blame me for a

prostitute getting pregnant, especially not when I went to such great lengths to make sure they all stayed on birth control and had regular access to condoms. But Manuel never needed a reason to blame me for anything.

"I… It's a Tuesday night. The girls can't possibly double the haul. Give me to the end of the week. I promise I'll make it happen."

"How old is River now? Remind me again?"

It wasn't a question. And I heard his threat loud and clear.

My eyes flared wide, bile climbing up the back of my throat. "I'll make it happen. Double the haul."

"Tonight," he seethed.

"Tonight. I swear."

I held the phone to my ear long after he'd hung up. I had no idea where I was going to get that money. Tuesdays only brought in around three grand, which—less the thirty percent the girls got to keep—left me in the hole for over two thousand dollars. If it was a Friday or Saturday, no problem. The girls took down ten times that on a weekend. But there was no fluffing the books on a Tuesday. Not to mention, I was already down four girls, Lucy—*poor fucking Lucy*—making it five.

"Shit," I muttered. This was going to be a big hit to my Freedom Account, but what other choice did I—

"I can get you that money."

My head popped up.

A perfect smile split her perfect face. "I wasn't lying. I got a rich guy on the hook."

"This hook big enough to dangle two grand off the tip?"

Her head snapped back with genuine surprise. "That's it?"

"That's it," I mocked, closing my eyes and pinched the bridge of my nose. "*Why* are you still here?"

"Because I'm thinking right now you need me. You give me four hours, I'll have that two grand for ya. Six and I can make it a cool three."

I pushed off the railing. "Generous offer, but what the hell would you get out of it?"

She turned her head away and whispered, "Protection."

My mouth gaped as I stared at her for several seconds. Then I let out a loud laugh. "Protection? Is that a joke?"

She pursed her lips. "Guerrero girls get respect, do they not?"

"Maybe on the street, but respect is a *big* word with a lot of meanings." I waved my arms around again, this time less like a *The Price is Right* model and more like an irate mother. "Within these walls, respect doesn't exist. And don't for one second think you will be different. Dante isn't interested in you modeling for him. The man doesn't even own a camera. He wants to whore you out, take seventy percent of your money, and then keep you captive in this building for the rest of your godforsaken life. So, if you have any concept of the word *respect*, you'll get gone. Take your two thousand dollars, get a fucking job that doesn't require you to lay on your back, and respect *yourself*. Now, if you will excuse me, I have shit to do." I stomped up the stairs, all of my patience exhausted.

"I still need Dante's number!" she called after me.

"Fuck. Off."

"I'm dead without it."

I froze, dropping my chin to my chest. She was dead if I gave it to her too.

I shouldn't have asked.

I shouldn't have cared.

I didn't even know her name.

And yet….

"Who are you running from?"

Her voice got closer as she spoke. "I swiped a couple bills off a guy. You know, just to get something to eat and… and, well, I need help. If I say I'm working for a Guerrero, he'll back off. I need that real bad."

I turned around. "So go to the cops."

"That shit doesn't work. You know that."

Unfortunately, I did. All too well.

"You have no idea what you are saying right now. Women don't come here to escape—they *leave* here to escape. Do you hear me? This isn't the place for safety."

She defiantly held my gaze. "Maybe not. But like your little word *respect*, safety is a big word with a lot of meanings. Let me decide for myself. Okay?"

I reached up, caught the star on my necklace, and dragged it back and forth across the chain. "Please don't make me do this."

She took a step up. "You'd be helping me out a lot. And I'll help you out too. I'll cut you in on whatever I take home each night. Fifty-fifty?"

"Your *cut* would be thirty percent. Guerreros get seventy. And then out of that thirty percent, you have to pay fifty percent to cover rent and utilities. So, out of that two thousand you're making tonight, you'll end the night with three-hundred bucks in your pocket."

"Okay, so you'd end up with seventy-five, then."

My chest ached. "I don't want your money."

She took another step up. "Okay. Then I can help in other ways. Whatever you need. I can do it."

"Jesus. Why are you so damn determined to do this? I'm giving you an out. *Take it*."

"There is no such thing as an out anymore. You got an out? What about the other girls here? They got an out? No. And whether you let me in here or not, I don't have an out, either."

I huffed a humorless laugh and planted a hand on my hip. "You do realize you're asking the devil for help, right?"

"At rock bottom, the devil's the only one left to help."

Wasn't that the damn truth.

I shook my head. "I'd have to clear this with Dante first."

"Okay."

Jesus, was I really going to do this? Girls were usually dropped off to me. And here I was, letting a new one in when I finally had the ability to tell her no.

"If I call him, there's no telling what he's going to say." I slid my gaze up her long, tan legs and over the swell of her large breasts.

She was gorgeous. If I called Dante, I knew *exactly* what he'd do to her. And it wasn't going to feel anything like safety.

"I know," she replied, hope sparkling in her eyes.

I held her stare, giving her every opportunity to stop

me as I lifted my phone.

She said nothing.

Finally, I dialed a number, but it wasn't Dante's.

"Why the fuck are you calling me right now?" Marcos greeted.

Short of Catalina, I had no friends in the Guerrero family. But when I needed something, Marcos was always my first call. He might hit me, but he didn't get his rocks off by fucking the girls. Marcos had a very specific type of woman he liked: the kind with a dick. Even if he'd never tell his family.

"*Last chance,*" I mouthed at her.

She smiled, folding her hands in front of her. "Please."

I sucked in a deep breath and then ruined her too. "Dante sent me over a girl."

"Andddd," he drawled impatiently.

"He didn't mention it. I'm just double-checking it's all good if I get her set up here."

Please say no. Please say no. Please say no.

"Woman, who made me your goddamn babysitter? Is she fuckable?"

I chewed on the inside of my cheek. "Yeah."

"Then let her fucking fuck!" He hung up.

I tucked the phone into my back pocket and tossed her a tight smile. "Welcome to the building..."

"Lexy," she filled in. "Lexy Palmer."

"Nice to meet you. I'm Cora Guerrero."

She gasped.

"Don't look at me like that. I'm only a Guerrero by marriage."

She gasped again, adding an eye bulge that made me laugh.

"And he passed away years ago."

"Oh, shit. I'm sorry."

"Don't worry about it. Just remember: I'm not one of them. Okay?"

"Okay." She smiled big, wide, breathtakingly, and... cluelessly.

Though, a few years later, it turned out I was the clueless one.

CHAPTER TWO

Cora

I n the two days since the fire, it felt like I was living in a state of suspended animation.

Time passed.

The world around me kept moving.

But I was equally lost and at the center of it all.

I remembered Drew ordering us delivery food a few times. I even vaguely remembered eating, though I couldn't have said what it was. It could have been Chinese just as easily as it could have been a burger.

It all tasted like misery.

"Cora, give it a rest for the night," Drew begged, sprawled out beside me on the bed. He'd been staying in the room with us since we got back.

"No," I clipped, clicking the restart button again. It stripped me bare every single time, but I couldn't stop watching.

I wasn't able to make out his face, but there was no doubting that it was him.

Penn in a black hoodie, going up the stairs.

Penn going into my apartment.

Penn coming out with his toolbox and heading down to his truck.

Dante and Marcos showing up.

Penn running up the stairs as Dante fired his gun, hitting him in the back of the leg.

Penn scrambling into my apartment.

More shots fired at the door until it swung open.

The Guerrero brothers filing inside.

No one ever coming back out.

I fast-forwarded six minutes until flames erupted from my apartment, the camera shaking violently before going black.

I moved the curser back to hover over the restart button, prepared to click again, but River's voice pulled me up short.

"Stop. You've seen it enough. You're just torturing yourself now."

I tore my gaze from the screen and gave her my attention. She'd been in the shower for the last hour. Her eyes were red rimmed, and the long, brown hair cascading over her shoulders caused wet circles to form on the front of her gray T-shirt.

We'd hit up Walmart on the way home from the building that first morning. I'd peeled off a grand of my Freedom Account and rushed inside to buy the necessities. The first being a laptop so I could watch the footage from Penn's secret security camera on something other than the cracked screen of my cell phone. I'd grabbed River a few things I thought she might need, but I'd been too frazzled to look at sizes. We'd only ended up with some baggy T-shirts and panties that were a size too small. I'd promised her I would take her back, but I hadn't been able to bring myself to leave the room yet.

The outside world felt too heavy without him.

"He's gone, River. It's torture either way."

She pursed her lips, a chin quiver escaping before she could hide it. "I know, but it doesn't matter how much you watch that video. It's not going to change."

Yeah. I wasn't the only one struggling with Penn's death.

"Come here, baby," I whispered, extending an arm in her direction.

"No! I don't want a hug. I want you to stop watching that damn video and figure out where we're going to live or when I can go back to school, or…or…or…what happens now if Manuel comes after us for this. You know he's going to find a way to blame you." She turned her fury on Drew. "And you… Jesus, it was your brother. He'll be coming after you too."

Drew sat up, placing both of his feet on the carpet and anchoring his elbows to his knees. "And it was Marcos and Dante who killed him. I'm not feeling particularly sympathetic toward Manuel tonight. Let him send someone after us. I dare him to try."

River stared at him, incredulous. "You get a two-for-one deal on Penn's coffin? Because that's where you're headed."

Drew opened his mouth, but I got there first.

"Okay, okay. Let's take it down a notch. We're all a little raw right now."

"Just put the damn computer down!" she yelled at me.

My back shot straight as I stared at her, tears filling our eyes. But before I could even contemplate the appropriate response, she raced back to the bathroom and slammed the door.

15

"Shit," I hissed. "Shit. Shit. Shit." My shoulders shook as I buried my face in my hands.

Drew was at my side in the next heartbeat. "Hey, shhhh." He rubbed a hand up and down my back. "She'll be okay."

"I don't think the word 'okay' is going to be in any of our vocabularies for a very long time."

He guided my head down to his shoulder. "But we gotta try."

My breathing stammered. "Why did he leave me and go to the building that night?"

"I don't know," he replied.

I sniffled and righted myself, glancing at the bathroom door when the sound of the shower made an encore. River was no doubt crying her eyes out in there. Damn kid was so stubborn that she wouldn't even let me comfort her.

Speaking of stubborn kids…

I cleared my throat and nabbed my phone off the bed. "I need to try the hospital again."

"Savannah's a minor. They're not going to tell you anything over the phone."

"Maybe not. But if I could get the right person on the phone, you never know. They might have a heart."

He moved back to his bed, muttering, "Yeah. Maybe."

I was searching for the hospital number again when my phone started ringing, my pulse skyrocketing when the word *unknown* flashed on the screen.

"Hello," I all but yelled.

"Holy shit, are you okay?" Catalina greeted.

My body crumbled as relief, agony, and adrenaline formed an earth-shattering combination inside me.

"No," I choked out, slapping a hand over my mouth.

"What the hell is going on? I just saw on the news. Are Marcos and Dante really dead?"

"Yeah," I whispered.

I had no idea how that was going to go over. She hated them, but they were still her brothers.

"What the hell happened?" she asked.

"I don't know. Honestly, I have no fucking idea." I glanced at Drew, who was swirling a paper cup of coffee and studiously pretending not to listen. After opening the drawer, I grabbed a few dollars off the top. "I'm gonna grab a pop," I told him and then pointed to the bathroom. "Keep an ear out for her."

He gave me curt nod, and I hurried out.

"Hey, you still there?" I asked, shutting the door, double-checking to make sure the lock had engaged.

"Yeah, I'm here," Cat replied. "I think I'm in shock though. I can't believe they're gone."

"I know. I'm sorry. I—"

"Sorry?" she snapped. "I'm about to plan a party. Cora, this is huge for us."

It did feel huge. But it didn't feel good. It burned like the hottest, sharpest knife slicing through me with methodical timing. Even in their death, they'd managed to punish me one last time.

"They killed Penn."

She cursed softly.

I swept my gaze through the hall, thankfully finding it empty. "Listen, something's not right here. It doesn't add up. Before the fire, Penn got into my safe, left his truck keys and a note that said, *One in. One out.* And he took down all the stars off my ceiling, Cat."

"Oh, wow."

"It gets weirder too. He left the stars in his truck, inside his toolbox, along with all of my pictures and important papers…and the money from the wall."

"What!" she gasped. "You got the money?"

I laughed, but it broke into a cry. "Oh, honey, you have no idea. I have *all* the money. Penn left me over a million dollars in cash."

"Wh… I'm sorry. What did you say?"

I ducked into the vending area when I heard a room door open nearby. I watched a happy couple, holding hands, meander to the elevator too lost in each other to notice I was there.

"You heard me. It was the exact amount, right down to the cent, that I told him I needed to get free of this life."

"You said he was the maintenance guy. Where did he get cash like that?"

"I have no idea. His brother, Drew, the one that was tight with your father in prison—he's just as clueless as I am."

"Don't you dare let that man try to get his hands on that money."

"He's not trying to take it!" I whisper-yelled. "He's sleeping on a bed next to me like a bodyguard. I have no idea what is going on right now. But something is seriously not right."

"Shit. Okay, let's breathe for a second and think this through. There's got to be an explanation. Maybe he was one of those secret millionaires."

"This is not a fucking movie!" I snapped. "Jesus, Cat. He

had motion sensor cameras in all the hallways. Drew said he installed them almost a month earlier, but Penn *never* mentioned it to me. I watched the video, and he very obviously carried my money out of the building in his toolbox. But where did the other money come from? It wasn't in his apartment. He didn't carry it down. It just magically appeared in the back seat of his truck.

"And it gets worse: The cops said it was an electrical fire in my apartment that started the blaze. But what the fuck? The amount of coincidence involved here is impossible. I'm supposed to believe that Penn *just so happened* to sneak out of my bed at the hotel and go back to the building where he *just so happene*d to pack up my money? And this was money that he wasn't even supposed to know existed. And then my stars? I never told him they were Nic's. But he thought they were important enough to peel them off the ceiling?

"And…and…and then your brothers *just so happened* to show up in the middle of the night and attacked him? I saw Dante shoot him in the leg before chasing him into *my apartment*. But what the hell happened after that? They didn't just all tuck in for the night and go to sleep. Even if it was pure coincidence that the fire started at that exact moment, why did none of them see it? Why did none of them try to get out?" I was panting by the time I finished.

"Maybe the fire wasn't a coincidence, then. Maybe one of them started the fire."

"Right!" I yelled, sans the whisper. "Okay, but which one of your dumbass brothers would have the first clue on how to rig an electrical fire? I'll tell you who could though… *Penn*. He rewired at least three apartments while he was there. But see, when the cops found their bodies..." My stomach rolled at the memory. "Penn was tied to chair."

"Shiiit," she breathed.

"Yet, again, I'm expected to believe that he *just so happened* to get everything that meant anything to me out of that building that night, then left me the exact amount of money I needed for me and all the girls to escape, and then the building caught fire, burning to the ground, taking the two men who kept me trapped for over half my life with it? *It just doesn't make sense.*"

"It's definitely suspect. But I'm not sure I'd be complaining. He basically solved all of your problems."

"But he died doing it." A rush of tears I should have long since run out of snuck up on me. "I want to know what happened to him. I loved him, Cat. I loved him so much. And I feel like he was another man who sacrificed everything for me. I don't know how to process that." I rested my forehead against the wall as two vending machines hummed behind me.

"You don't have to process it, Cora. Not right now, anyway. Grieve. Be sad. Cry. Fine. But you don't have to figure it out. What are the cops saying?"

I took a few seconds to collect myself before answering. "Nothing really. I think they were just happy to finally be rid of Marcos and Dante. You know the cops haven't been their biggest fans since Manuel went down."

"They aren't the only ones," she muttered to herself. "Good. At least they aren't looking at you for any of this. And what about Penn's brother? Have you talked to him about this?"

Another room door opened, and I peeked into the hall and saw Drew heading my way as if his ears had been burning. I got busy straightening out dollar bills on the side of the pop machine and whispered, "I don't know. I think he's still in shock. He keeps saying stupid crap, like maybe Penn was trying to take off with all that money. But Penn clearly left everything for me to find."

I'd only fed one bill into the machine before Drew rounded the corner.

"Shit. There you are. How long does it take to get a drink? I was starting to worry."

I swiped under my eyes and offered him a halfhearted smile. "Sorry. I just needed a minute alone." I pointed at the phone. "It's Brittany. I was talking to her about getting the girls together so I can give them some money."

His eyebrows gathered. "Right. Of course."

"I'll be back in a minute. Okay?" I lifted the dollar in his direction. "You want anything?"

"Nah. I'm good." Skeptically, he stared at me for another beat. Then he shook his head and reluctantly backed away.

I leaned through the doorway and watched until he was out of earshot. "Listen, I need a way to get in touch with you. Things are different now. We don't have to sneak around anymore."

"Well, maybe not from my brothers, but my father and Thomas are still very much alive."

"I just need a number, Cat. I'll keep it private."

"Okay. Okay. I'll text it over."

"Thank you," I whispered. "Now, I've got to go. I'm going to see what info I can get out of Drew. I'll keep you updated if anything comes up. Oh, and stay away from the storage unit. That's where I ditched the cash."

"Jesus. A million dollars. Seriously?"

My stomach pitched as I added, "And ninety-nine cents."

She sighed. "Okay. I love you. One in. One out. Remember?"

"Always," I breathed before hanging up.

I finished up at the machine, getting River a Mountain Dew that I hoped would serve as some sort of treat/peace offering. As I walked back to the room, I called Brittany and asked her to get up to the hotel as soon as possible.

If I wanted to keep Drew in the dark, I was going to have to be a little more convincing.

CHAPTER THREE

Penn

My hands ached at my sides as I watched him exit the courthouse.

He was smiling, carefree and oblivious, while chatting it up with the herd of well-dressed men hanging on his every word. From his tailored, navy-pinstriped suit down to his perfectly styled dark-brown hair, the man looked every bit the successful prosecutor the city knew him to be.

But I knew he was so much more than that.

Thomas Lyons was a soulless bastard who I would make damn sure followed his old friends Marcos and Dante into an early grave.

The hot summer wind wrapped around me, fanning the fire in my soul. There wasn't much I could do right then. Not in such a public place. And not without the time or the space to make him properly suffer. A quick and painless death was not at all what I had planned for him.

Twenty-nine minutes had destroyed me.

Twenty-nine minutes of her screams of agony.

Twenty-nine minutes he had arranged.

No. Thomas Lyons would pay tenfold for each and every

one of those minutes.

But waiting for the right moment to make a move wasn't proving to be easy, either.

His every breath taunted me, knowing that his heart was still pumping blood through his worthless veins while hers was rotting on a stained piece of carpet in a garbage pile somewhere.

She was dead.

And he was smiling.

My vision flashed red as he stopped at the bottom of the concrete steps to talk to a younger woman. She too was in a suit, though hers was punctuated with a pair of heels and a black leather briefcase at her side. A colleague perhaps.

But all I saw was Lisa.

She'd been fearless the day I'd met her. Knowing that crazy woman, she'd probably marched right up to Thomas, her Louboutins I'd worked my ass off to provide for her clicking the sidewalk, and dropped the bomb about all the dirt she'd dug up on him. She would have wanted to witness firsthand the shock contorting his face. She'd have reveled in the glint of fear appearing in his eyes.

Lisa was a good person with a wicked addiction to justice. There was no standing in her way. God knew, I'd tried, but I'd never been able to argue her out of anything. She hadn't cared what it cost or how much she had to go through to make it happen.

Her heart had been set on making the world a better place.

Even as it beat for the very last time.

Pain from the graze of Dante's bullet at my calf made me

wince as I moved to stay out of Thomas's line of sight. Not that he would have recognized me. Our worlds had collided, but he and I had never crossed paths.

At least not yet.

I casually propped my back against the brick wall outside the local coffee shop, my stomach churning as he grinned down at the woman and his hand cradled her at the elbow as he bent to touch his lips to her cheek. It was chaste enough to be friendly, but the way she swayed into him was anything but.

This fucking piece of shit. Murder aside, he had a wife who was so terrified of him that she'd taken their daughter and run. And he was making moves—or, at the very least, eyes—at a woman who had to be twenty years his junior.

My hands began to ache all over again.

"Is that him?" Savannah whispered in my ear.

"Shit!" I growled, wheeling around and nearly knocking the cup of coffee out of her hand.

"Shit," she parroted, teetering to the side.

I snaked a hand out, catching her before she toppled over. "Jesus, kid."

"Don't Jesus me. You were the one who randomly turned into the bumbling Hulk. Here." She extended a paper cup of coffee my way, keeping the iced-fru fru-chocolate-whatever for herself.

I turned back around in time to see Thomas and the woman walking away together.

"He's not attractive," Savannah announced around the straw of her drink.

Curling my lip, I shot her a glare over my shoulder. "Are

you kidding me right now?"

Her red, penciled eyebrows shot up. "What? I was just making an observation."

Starting toward the car, I gave her my back. "Well, keep your *observations* to yourself. That man is a piece of shit masquerading as salt of the Earth. I don't give the first damn what he looks like. All I care about is how fast I can take him down."

"Jeez. Forget I said anything." She scoffed, following after me.

She'd been with me for two days.

Two *excruciating* days.

She wasn't a bad kid. Truth be told, she was a really fucking good kid, with a good heart and a troubled soul her parents had never taken the time to heal. However, when I looked at her, all I saw was Cora. Not in her features or her mannerisms, but rather in my memories. And considering that it had only been a little over a week, those memories were still so fresh and so potent that they wrecked me every time.

I missed Cora something fierce. And with her out there, hurting, it was a wonder I could function at all.

But I'd done all I could for her.

I'd cashed out a substantial portion of my retirement account to leave her that million and change, but where I was going, money in the bank didn't matter. Though, if I was being honest, it had never truly mattered.

It hadn't saved Lisa.

It hadn't kept me from falling into the darkness after she'd died.

But I hoped like hell it could save Cora.

There was a good chance Drew was never going to speak to me again. Giving her the cash was always supposed to be the backup plan if anything truly happened to me. But when I'd gotten to the building that night, I'd peered up at the railing on the third floor, imagining her smile as she stared down at me the way she so often did when I got home from a run.

Leaving her was going to destroy me in ways from which I'd never recover.

But I couldn't walk away without knowing she had everything I could possibly give her.

However, that meant taking some things from her as well.

That building. That fucking building. It had been her home for over a decade.

But it had to go.

I couldn't risk that they would ever try to take her back there. Manuel had at least another five years on his sentence, but his empire would not still be standing when he walked out of the chain link gates.

The biggest part of that legacy was his family name.

So, one after the other, I choked the life out of his sons as well.

In the previous four years, I'd done a lot of things in the name of avenging Lisa's death.

But that.

Killing Dante and Marcos.

That was for Cora.

And I would never feel the first regret over it.

So yeah, while I hated knowing that Cora was hurting,

I was able to climb out of bed, put one foot in front of the other, and breathe through the pain of losing her all because I knew she was free.

Drew was going to stay with her until she got settled somewhere new.

I'd like to think he was doing it as a favor to me.

I knew Drew though. He liked to play the hard-ass, but he was a good guy who cared about Cora more than he'd ever admit. He'd make sure she was taken care of.

Even if I couldn't.

Savannah and I climbed into my car, my door slamming while hers softly clicked.

"Are we gonna follow him?" she asked.

I ground my teeth, hating like hell that she was involved in this clusterfuck. But the moment I'd let her climb into my car that night, I'd made her a part of this. I shouldn't have picked her up. I should have called Drew, told him where she was, and let him handle it.

But I'd promised Cora I'd get her back. Hell, I'd driven seven hours to Cleveland using the little details I'd gathered about Savannah over my two months with Cora to track her down.

And seeing her standing on that corner, with bruises on her arms, clearly up to no good, I couldn't wait.

She needed help.

And I was there.

Well...Shane Pennington was there. I didn't know who the fuck *I* was anymore.

When she'd asked questions about Cora, I'd been forced to tell her the truth.

Or at least part of it.

I'd glossed over Lisa. Then told her that Marcos and Dante were dead, but I didn't explain the how, i.e. me being responsible. This led us to the fire at the building, then the money I left behind, and finally the body Drew had purposely identified as my own.

For being sixteen, she'd taken all of it surprisingly well. Her first question had been a shrieked, "Holy shit. You left her a million dollars?" Followed by, "Holy shit. Where'd you get a million dollars?" Followed by, "Holy shit. Can I have a million dollars?" But after she'd calmed down, her face had paled as she'd whispered, "The whole building is gone?" Followed by, "Were any of the girls hurt?" Followed by, "Cora thinks you're dead?"

Her heartbreaking concern was nothing compared to the hurricane swirling inside me, but I had only one answer. "Yeah. And no matter what happens, you can't tell her I'm alive. She'll become a target, Savannah. I left so she could finally have a life of her own, not get bogged down in someone else's shit. After everything she's done, I think we can both agree she deserves that much."

She nodded, I nodded, and then we rode the first three hours back to Chicago in silence, both of us lost in our own thoughts.

The fourth hour was spent *not* in silence after she had what I could only explain as a vocal seizure when I snatched her phone mid-text and threw it out the window south of Ann Arbor. I told her I'd replace it. She glanced around the car, no doubt remembering the money I'd left Cora, and then demanded the latest and greatest iPhone. I laughed and told her she was funny.

She'd fumed for a solid hour, but then she'd fallen asleep and slept for the last two.

Those were my favorite of the trip because, for those two hours, it had been easy to forget how bad everything had gotten.

Cora and River were safe with Drew.

Savannah was safe with me.

And for one more night, as the headlights illuminated that seemingly endless highway, I pretended I was still drowning and not already at the bottom of the ocean.

Now, watching Savannah out of the corner of my eye as she slurped her coffee, I felt that same sense of contentment slithering through me. If only Cora had been there too.

Cora.

Cora.

Cora.

My mind's favorite distraction.

And torture.

I sucked in a deep breath, holding it until my lungs ached. On an exhale, I answered, "No. We're not following him."

"Why not? He's so close."

I turned into traffic the opposite direction than Thomas had wandered off. "Because you're with me. I don't want you involved in this. I shouldn't have brought you down here to get coffee today. Speaking of…" I snapped my finger and put my hand out palm up. "Change. I gave you a fifty."

"Oh, come on! It's, like, thirty bucks. What if I need something? I don't even have money to catch a cab back to your apartment."

"A cab?" I flashed her a glare. "I'm not sure if you realize this, but the thing you're sitting in right now, it's more than just a beautiful piece of German machinery. It's actually a car too."

My gaze was aimed at the road, but I didn't have to see her to know she was rolling her eyes.

"I mean, if we're not together, Penn. You still haven't replaced my phone." She pouted her bottom lip and batted her painted-black lashes at me. "I'd be all alone out there with no way to get back to you, Papa."

"You call me Papa again and I'm gonna ground you for the rest of your life."

She laughed, throwing her head back against the seat. "Daddy? Is that any better?"

"God. No."

"Okay, cool. You're right. We'll keep it simple and stick with dad."

I slowed at a stoplight and angled to look at her. Her wild, red hair was up in one of those messy piles on the top of her head that River so often sported. But do not be mistaken; it had taken her at least twenty minutes in front of the mirror to get that thing messy without being *too messy*.

I'd forgotten what it was like to live with a woman. Cora was as low maintenance as it got. If her blond curls weren't cascading down her back, they were pulled back in a rubber band she permanently wore around her wrist. This styling action was usually performed while she was walking, talking, or, on occasion, riding my...

Shit. I had to stop thinking about her.

Savannah. That's what I needed to focus on.

The day after we'd gotten home from Cleveland, I'd taken her shopping. What this really meant is I'd taken her to the mall where we'd argued over clothes, she'd ended up storming out, and I'd ultimately thrown a pile of what I'd deemed to be age-appropriate attire—even though she'd deemed it all "hideous"—beside the cash register along with my credit card. She'd only started speaking to me again when I'd handed her my card and agreed to stand outside as she hit Victoria's Secret. I didn't give a fuck what she wore *under* her clothes as long as they weren't visible.

"How about we stick with you calling me *Penn*, and then you actually give me back my change? We agreed no money, no phone, no nothing until we get you into some kind of drug program."

"No. *You* agreed to that." She dug into the pocket of her entirely-too-short cut-off jeans—the severed legs more than likely sitting on the floor in my guest bedroom—and slapped a wadded ball of cash and coins onto my hand. "I told you I don't need a program. I've been clean for months."

I arched an eyebrow. "Truth?"

Her lips thinned before she turned away from me to peer out the window, muttering, "Not including the shit Dante gave me."

"I'm not talking about that. Once you got out of the hospital, you haven't touched anything. No weed. No coke. No nothing. Truth, Savannah?" The light turned green and I dumped the cash into a cup holder before easing on the gas.

"You don't know what it's like out there," she whispered.

I forced my hands to stay on the steering wheel. It didn't

feel right to touch her, not when she was trusting me enough to drop her guard. It was rare she showed any kind of vulnerability, and I personally hadn't seen any since the day she'd flipped out on Cora for not sleeping with me yet.

Annnnd we were back to Cora.

Shit. I had to focus.

"No," I replied. "I don't know what it's like. And I'm not claiming I do. But I do know how incredible you are when you're clean. You're smart, Savannah. And funny. And bright. And beautiful in ways that have nothing to do with your clothes or makeup. But none of that matters if you're letting drugs ruin the kind of perfect you already are. You've dealt with some shit, kid. I do not fault you one bit for anything you've done in the past. But, now, it's time to change. And I told you I'd help with that, and I don't particularly care if you *agreed* or not. Because I see something in you, whether you see it in yourself or not."

Her face got tight, but as I divided my attention between her and the road, I saw the tears sliding down her cheeks.

She hurried to dry them—just like someone else I knew. And couldn't stop thinking about.

"Jeez. What is this, an after school special?"

I smiled. "What do you know about after school specials? Isn't that, like, thirty years before your time?"

"Public school education, Penn. Kids twenty years from now will still be watching those things in health class."

I chuckled, and then we both fell quiet again. I'd spent so much of the last four years praying for the silence and hoping people would leave me alone. But right then, with no clue as to what was going through her head, it bothered me.

"You know I'm only trying to help, right?"

"Yeah, I know," she told the window.

The trip back to my apartment was a short one. The first time we'd pulled into the underground parking garage, Savannah had had another vocal seizure, exclaiming, "Holy shit! You live here?" This time, though, she didn't say anything as we rode the elevator up to my three-bedroom, four-thousand-square-foot, sixth-floor apartment.

It was overkill. Completely and totally. I'd had no reason to buy a place that big, or nice, or permanent. I didn't need it. Deep down, I really just wanted to go back to that shitty building and crawl into Cora's bed again. Maybe lie there for the rest of my life, alternating between playing Truth or Lie tit-for-tat, listening to her laugh, and making love to her.

Yet, when I'd seen pictures of that apartment online, all I could see was Cora.

Her bare feet padding against the dark wood floor—not a speck of carpet anywhere in sight—as she meandered from the bedroom wearing nothing but one of my button-downs.

Her sleepy smile as she navigated around the large marble island to get to me.

Her arms wrapping around my hips and her face nuzzling against my chest, making me feel more corporeal than I had in my entire life.

Her soft lips brushing mine when she pressed up onto her toes for an all-too-brief kiss before snagging the coffee cup from my hand.

Her sigh as she tipped it back like the caffeine had touched her soul.

Peaceful. Content. Blissed out beyond all explanation.

Cora would never even see that apartment, but with that scenario playing in my head as I'd scrolled through pictures, I'd cleared out another hefty portion of my retirement and bought it—fully furnished—on the spot.

And it was that exact scene that assaulted me when Savannah and I walked inside, the beeping of the security alarm acting as our welcoming committee.

Only, like a rainstorm of razorblades, Cora was nowhere to be found.

And the constant reminder that she never would be was suffocating.

Savannah stepped out of her tall wedges in the middle of the foyer, never breaking her gait as she kept walking.

"Um, hello. Shoes," I scolded, tapping in a series of numbers into the security panel.

I listened for her huff, maybe an exaggerated groan. She didn't even acknowledge that I'd spoken.

"Hey!" I called as she disappeared down the hall.

Christ. Teenage girls were a breed of their own.

Kicking her shoes out of the way, I continued into the expansive living room and promptly collapsed onto the chocolate leather sofa. It was not even noon, but I felt like it was midnight. Not surprisingly, I hadn't been sleeping well. My mind was a jumbled mess of guilt, resentment, and revenge.

But I had shit to do. I couldn't lie there all day and lose myself the way I so desperately wanted.

Sucking in, I angled up only to stop when Savannah reappeared with a bowl of water and a white grocery sack dangling from her fingers. She'd changed into pink-polka-dot pajama pants and a matching oversized T-shirt I'd picked out for her. Just the day before, she'd told me that they belonged on a six-year-old and threatened to burn them.

"Sit," she ordered, perching on the edge of the coffee table. She set the bowl beside her and started tearing open gauze, prepping it with antibiotic cream.

In the last ten minutes, she'd cried, cracked a joke, and ignored me.

She'd never apologize. But this, wearing clothes she hated while offering to take care of the wound on my leg, was her olive branch.

I still needed to figure out how to get her a new birth certificate so I could check her into a treatment program. I'd highly underestimated the documentation needed to get a minor medical help. Hell, I had no idea how Cora had registered her in school. According to my research online, I needed everything including a vial of blood and a sacrificial goat to get her enrolled again.

But all of that shit could wait one more day.

And for that reason alone, I folded up the leg of my jeans and propped my boot on the table beside her.

CHAPTER FOUR

Cora

"No," I snapped.

"What do you mean *no*? You gave five grand to Jennifer. And I get two hundred bucks?" Meredith asked, thoroughly insulted.

"You got two hundred bucks *and* a trip to rehab," I corrected. "When you finish there and stay clean for another thirty days of outpatient, I'll pay for a plane ticket for you to go to your sister's house in Virginia. And when you get a job that actually requires you to pay taxes and stay clean for another thirty days, I'll pay your first and last months' rent on an apartment of your own."

"That's not fair!" she shouted, looking around the room for someone to back her up.

Jennifer was not surprisingly silent. Tears were still streaming down her cheeks after hearing the news that I—or, really, Penn—was going to pay for her first year of college, and I'd given her five grand to buy a car and a wardrobe with slightly more fabric.

"Meredith, I'm gonna tell you this one more time and then, if you keep this shit up, you are walking out of here with nothing. I am not here to fund your life. I am here to make sure you live long enough to actually have one. So take the damn money. Go buy a toothbrush and some body wash, and I'll text you the details on the rehab program I find for you. It's your choice if you want to show up or not. But if you don't, then this will be the last money you ever get off me. Do you understand?"

She was so pissed that her face was turning red.

I couldn't have cared less.

Penn had died to get them that money. If they didn't want it, I'd give it to someone who did. Cut and dry. End of story.

I waved the two hundred bucks in her direction. "Last chance."

"This is bullshit," she muttered, but she plucked the money from between my fingers and stomped out.

I wasn't sure if she'd take me up on my rehab offer, but she needed it. Desperately. She'd been using drugs and alcohol to numb the pain for too long.

And with absolute agony burning my soul, I understood her more than ever. But I didn't have the ability to fall into the pits of despair like so many of the girls had over the years.

I had to keep going.

Keep moving.

Keep…living.

Even when I couldn't breathe.

One in. One out.

"Thanks, Cora," Jennifer said softly before giving me a hug.

"No problem. Get those applications in as soon as

possible, and let me know where you get accepted."

She nodded, more tears falling from her chin.

"And stop crying. You deserve this. You're smart, Jenn. Just keep your head up, and I know you'll kick some major college ass."

"I promise. I will."

"Now, get out of here. You have some shopping to do."

She nodded again and started out, but Drew stopped her short of the door.

"You find a car you're interested in, you call me and I'll come take a look at it before you buy it. Used-car salesmen love nothing more than to rip off an unsuspecting woman."

She smiled up at him. "Thanks, Drew."

He offered her a wink, but there was nothing flirty about it. It was sweet.

With the exception of going back and forth to the storage unit to grab me more cash and the occasional dinner, he hadn't left our sides since the fire. I wasn't sure if he was using us as a distraction to escape the reality that he'd really lost his brother. Or maybe he was genuinely worried about me and stayed to keep his finger on the pulse. Either way, it was nice having him around.

At first.

For the last week, we'd all been in a holding pattern. The sun rose every morning and set every night, but that was the only thing that seemed normal anymore. Everything else was foreign territory.

Life without the chaos of running the building.

Life without the fear of Marcos and Dante.

Life without the warmth of Penn's arms.

I was still confused on what had actually happened that night. I'd asked Drew a million different questions, but he didn't seem to have any answers. Or at least none that he was telling me.

He'd sworn that he didn't know where the money had come from.

And promised me that he had no idea why Penn had been at the apartment.

He'd looked me right in the eyes and vehemently told me he was just as confused as I was.

But he wasn't, because he hadn't spent the last week asking me the exact same questions.

People by nature seek the answers to what we don't understand. Especially when it comes to our loved ones. When Nic had been murdered, I'd been there and *still* sought an explanation from the Guerreros for the events that had led up to his death.

While Drew definitely seemed affected by having lost Penn, he wasn't consumed with grief.

The police had been by the hotel multiple times to talk to Drew. He'd always step out into the hall or meet them down in the lobby. At first, I'd thought it was because he was shielding me from more pain.

But, more recently, I was getting suspicious that maybe he was actually shielding me from the truth.

I'd had my fair share of conversations with the cops too, but they didn't seem to have any more answers than I did.

After Manuel had gone to jail on a laundry list of convictions, the police had been eyeing Marcos and Dante for years. They were suspects one and two when the city's famed district attorney, Thomas Lyons, had reported his wife and his child as missing—this bullshit including a tear-filled press conference that made primetime news. Back then, I'd figured that had been the equivalent of declaring World War III. And while I would have loved nothing more than for Thomas to finish what he'd started and take down the rest of the Guerrero family, surprisingly, he'd never followed through. He had the power, but I suspected he enjoyed the national attention, and the mystery of it all definitely hadn't hurt his career. The label of "grieving victim" had only made his parade of justice that much more impressive while he'd single-handedly plowed through the city's criminal population.

The cops had never let Catalina's disappearance go, and watching Thomas, who they considered one of their own, lose his family had only painted a bigger target on the Guerreros' backs. But they'd never gotten anything to stick on either one of them. Now though, with a video of Marcos and Dante chasing a man into an apartment, that man being my boyfriend and me being their dead brother's wife, it wasn't like they were spending a lot of time trying to prove the Guerreros' innocence.

Especially not after a search of their houses revealed a fresh body buried in Marcos's backyard and over a million dollars' worth of drugs in Dante's house. As far as the police were concerned, everything was tied up in a pretty red bow for them. Case closed.

As for me, I was more concerned with the *how* this had happened.

Dante and Marcos's official cause of death had come back as smoke inhalation, but they'd suffered significant trauma to their faces and their bodies before that. The cops had concluded that it was from fighting with Penn inside the apartment before the fire had broken out.

Meanwhile, Penn's official cause of death had been ruled a homicide thanks to a bullet in his chest.

I'd thrown up for over an hour after Detective Morris had informed us of this.

Even in a state of total emotional upheaval, I kept a close eye on Drew.

He was Penn's *brother*, after all. His only response had been to let out a loud curse, thank the detective, and then sit on the floor in the bathroom with me, alternating between rubbing my back and staring at his shoes. It was strange. But everyone handled emotions differently.

Then it got weirder. Drew was still waiting on the city to release Penn's body, and over the last few days, I'd started planning a small memorial ceremony. I'd never seen Drew so mad as when I'd told him about it. He'd stormed out of the room and sat in the hall with his forearms propped on his knees and his head hanging between his arms for over two hours. I may have (read: definitely) watched him through the peephole for at least half of that time. He didn't speak as he crawled into bed that night. And the next day, he didn't mention it at all.

Yeah. It was safe to say something was *definitely* not right. And while I hadn't yet been able to figure it out, I wasn't about to give up.

As the days passed, my patience was slipping with Drew. But if there was one thing I'd learned in the thirteen years since Nic died, it was that anger got me nowhere. However, an unassuming smile and a well-thought-out plan? Yeah. I was in business.

"Anyone else coming today?" Drew asked, flipping the lock on the top of the door after Jennifer left.

I sat beside River on the bed. She moved the laptop to her other side to allow me space.

I shot him an appreciative grin. "No, it was just those two today. How much are we down to?"

He pulled his phone out, his fingers swiping across the screen on what I assumed was the calculator. "I guess depending on how much college costs these days, a little over six hundred left."

I groaned. I had so much to do. I wasn't eager to give any of the girls a ton of cash. It'd be all too easy for them to get robbed or blow it twenty dollars at a time until they had nothing left. Instead, I was paying as much as I could to businesses, apartment complexes, colleges, doctors, and, soon, a few different rehab facilities. Seeing as to how this all had to be done via cash transaction, it was incredibly time consuming.

But staying busy was far better than the stabbing pain I felt each time I thought about everything we'd lost.

River looked up at me. "You're really just going to give away all this money?"

"You got a better idea?"

She turned the computer to face me. "Yeah. We find an apartment that costs more than seven hundred bucks a month. These places aren't much better than the last one."

"Baby, we have over a million dollars in cash and I have a record and no job. If we get anything that costs more than seven hundred dollars a month, we might as well hang a red flag on the door ourselves. Besides, you just gonna forget about everybody else? What do you think will happen to them next? Dante is gone, but that doesn't mean that someone else isn't waiting to take his place. And who knows? Maybe that guy is worse. We take care of each other. That means me and you. And us and them."

She shifted uncomfortably and flicked her gaze back to the screen. "Okay. I'll keep looking."

I tossed my arm around her shoulders. "I'll tell you what. I'll bump it up to seven fifty. Does that make it any easier?"

She started scrolling through apartment listings again. "Nah, seven hundred's good. We'll be fine."

God, she was a good kid.

Drew settled on the bed beside us, grabbed the remote, and aimed it at the TV. "So what are we doing tonight, ladies? You want to rent a movie or something?"

"Why don't you go out?" I suggested.

His head snapped my way. "You trying to get rid of me?"

Yes, I thought.

"Maybe," I teased.

His jaw slacked open with mock injury, but before he had the chance to reply, a loud knock sounded at the door.

The humor in his face disappeared as he asked, "You expecting anyone?"

I shook my head, panic erupting inside me. River must have felt it, because she set the computer aside and sat up.

He knifed up off the bed and walked to the door, breathing a curse before pulling it open. "Detective Morris, how can I—"

"Where's Cora?"

I flew up off the bed, my heart lurching into my throat as the detective—flanked by two uniformed officers—entered the room.

The detective's dark-brown gaze shot over my shoulder. "River Guerrero?"

"Yeah?" she drawled.

One of the uniforms advanced on her, muttering a, "We got her," into the radio at his shoulder.

Spreading my arms wide as though I could hide her, I cut him off. "You got who? What is this about?"

The detective's gaze flicked back to mine. "You need to come with me. Both of you. Now."

River hit my back, her body already shaking. My heart thundered in my ears as I intertwined her hand with mine.

"Why?" I asked, scanning the room. The hair on the back of my neck stood on end as the officers continued to close in. "What's going on?"

He planted his hands on his hips and uncomfortably shifted his gaze away. I didn't know Detective Morris well by any means, but I'd seen him enough over the last week to be on a somewhat friendly basis with him. He'd been kind each time we'd spoken, gentle as though he almost felt bad for me.

And the nerves in my stomach peaked when I got the distinct feeling that he didn't want to be there any more than I wanted him to be.

"We have a warrant for your arrest, Cora. I'm going to ask you to kindly step away from the child and come with me."

My lungs seized as my hands started to tremble. "Wh… what for?"

"What?" Drew growled behind him, but I couldn't find him in the suddenly crowded room.

"Child endangerment," Morris said. "Now, you come without trouble and I won't cuff you in front of the kid."

"Mom!" River cried, the fear in her voice slicing me to the bone.

"It's okay," I replied as a knee-jerk reaction. It clearly was *not* okay. But, then again, it never had been and we'd survived all the same. "What kind of endangerment?"

One of the uniformed officers made a move to grab River's arm, and I stepped to the side to block him.

"Wait. Wait. Wait." I lifted my palms. "I haven't done anything wrong."

Morris cut his gaze away. "And you can explain that to a judge. But, for now, I need River to go with Officer DeSalva and you to come with me." He pointedly tipped his chin over my shoulder and the other uniformed officer stepped in, catching River by the back of the arm.

She started crying as they pulled her away, and each tear struck me like the hottest branding iron. She'd been through so much in her thirteen years. We'd never had the cops show up and take her away before, but watching her being dragged out of my reach wasn't something new for either of us.

But this wasn't last time.

This was different. We weren't trapped by the Guerreros anymore.

I was free.

We were supposed to be free.

"Mom!" she called as they carted her toward the door, her brown eyes anchored to me over her shoulder.

"Relax, baby. It's going to be okay," I lied, hoping I could make it the truth. "Just go with the officer and I'll see you in a little while. I promise."

The panic in her eyes shredded me as she disappeared out the door.

As soon as she was gone, the second uniformed officer moved in on me, painfully wrenching my arms as he forced my hands behind my back. The cool metal of his cuffs cinched tight around my wrists, biting into my flesh. But my mind was too busy trying to figure out my next move to give the pain any weight.

"Drew? Drew?" I yelled, bordering on the verge of hysterics.

"I'm right here, Cor," he replied from the hallway, where he was standing with two other cops.

Jesus. They'd sent four cops and a detective? That should have been the moment I heard the alarm bells. They had known exactly where I was and I'd been more than cooperative all week, yet they'd sent *four* cops and a detective after me like I'd been holding River at gunpoint. But I was too focused on how I was going to get River back to even consider the whys.

"I need you to find me an attorney," I told Drew. "A good one, okay?"

His face was hard as stone as he glared at the cop roughly forcing me down the hall, but he gave me a curt nod and clipped, "I'm on it."

"Please. Hurry," I breathed.

"Cora Guerrero?" the cop called.

"That's me!" I said, shooting off the bench in the holding cell and rushing toward the door.

"Hands," he ordered.

As he clicked the cuffs in place, I asked, "Can you tell me where my daughter is?"

"Nope. Now, stop talking."

My stomach dropped. I was growing more nervous by the minute. I'd been there for well over three hours without any word on River or my attorney.

"Is my attorney here yet? I'd really like to talk to him."

"As a matter of fact, he is," he replied.

I blew out a shaky breath, intoxicating relief surging through my veins. "Oh, thank God." But I couldn't stop worrying about where they'd taken River.

By most people's standards, the life I'd given her wasn't great, but at least I loved her.

With my entire being.

I always made sure she was taken care of. Yes, she came from a family of criminals, but I'd taught her the difference between right and wrong. And when she had been little, I always took her to doctors' appointments and got all of her shots on time. Now that she was older, I couldn't afford braces or anything, but she'd never had a cavity. Every night she'd watched all the girls head out to work, I'd fought like hell to make sure she understood that she was worth so much more than just her body. I'd never wanted that life for her. So I'd spent every minute, every resource, and every opportunity I'd had preparing her for bigger and better things than I'd ever been able to provide her with.

I was far from a perfect mother, but I tried.

Every single day.

And while I agreed wholeheartedly that she deserved better than that, I knew that the foster care system wasn't ever going to give her more than I could. I'd had too many girls come through my building eighteen and fresh out of the system to ever believe otherwise.

The police officer slowed to a stop at the end of the hall and then shoved a door on my left open. "Inside." He didn't follow me in.

Short of a table and two chairs, the room was empty. There were no windows, no double-sided mirrors. It wasn't like anything I'd experienced in past arrests.

It was just a white room bleached of all color—and hope.

"Sit down. I'll be right back." He let the door quietly swoosh shut, not even clicking it locked behind him.

Searching for a camera or any sign of outside life, I walked over and used my toe to slide the chair out before sinking down.

My leg bounced up and down as I waited. Out of habit, I reached for the star around my neck only to remember they'd taken it from me when they'd processed me in. I had two strikes against me, but assuming no drugs had climbed into my pockets of their own volition, I should have been okay.

It was false confidence like that that made the blow of seeing his face appear in the doorway feel like a knock-out punch.

"Hello, Cora," Thomas Lyons drawled as he sauntered into the room.

He had visibly aged since the last time I'd seen him. I couldn't remember exactly how much older than Catalina he was, but flecks of gray now showed in his dark-brown hair. His blue eyes were friendly enough to make him approachable, but I knew all too well how bottomless his soul truly was.

He opened the button on his suit coat as he sat down. My attention was drawn to the wedding ring he was still wearing on his left hand. But it was all for show. Thomas was an attention whore in the worst way.

"What the hell are you doing here?" I asked.

He grinned, full of arrogance. "I heard the cops picked you up. I thought maybe you needed some legal expertise."

I buried my hands in my lap so he couldn't see them tremble. "You heard? Or sent them after me?"

He shrugged, turning to the side to cross his legs knee over knee like the pretentious prick he was. "Potato. Patahto. All that matters is I'm here to get you out."

Negative amounts of hope hit my chest. Thomas had never done anything out of the kindness of his heart in his entire life. He wasn't about to start with me.

"Oh, yeah? And what's it going to cost me?"

His eyes narrowed, but his smile never faltered. "Where is she, Cora?"

My pulse thundered in my ears, but I showed him

nothing. "I have no idea who you're talking about."

"Right. Of course you don't." He intertwined his fingers and cradled them around the top of his knee. "But let's speak hypothetically here. Let's pretend for a second that there is a certain child who may or may not be in grave danger. See, her mother is a prostitute with several drug convictions on her record, and more than once, she has had the aforementioned child taken away from her. What do you think would happen if, let's say, a concerned uncle who also happens to be a man of many powers called in a favor to have the child permanently removed from the mother's care?"

My lungs burned as the air in that room became toxic, but I held his stare and refused my eyes the tears they were calling to the surface. "Well, hypothetically of course, it sounds like that concerned uncle is making quite a few assumptions about the mother and is trying to control a situation he knows absolutely nothing about. If I had to guess, I'd say he was probably compensating for some *personal inadequacies*, if you know what I mean. However, if I were that mother, which, clearly I'm not, seeing as you mentioned that she was a prostitute, my advice to her would be to stop talking to the asshole and wait for her attorney."

He laughed. "You mean Frank Esposito? Yeah, I saw him out front. That man is a beast when it comes to family law."

Oh, thank God. Drew had come through.

"Right. Then please direct all further hypothetical games his way."

"I sent him home."

I shot to my feet, the chair falling over behind me. "You can't do that!"

"Cora, honey. Frank and I play golf every weekend. What do you expect?"

I expected that, for once in my life, someone would actually help me—even if I had to pay them to do it. I should have known better. The law was only fair when everyone followed the same rules.

He rose from his seat and prowled around the table. Panic exploded inside me, and I tried to scramble away, but the room was too small to allow me any space. My back hit the wall as his hand found my throat.

"Stop," I hissed, clawing at his wrist, but it only made him tighten his grip until breathing became an impossible task. Frantic, I glanced to the door, begging for someone to walk by. But even if they did, I wasn't sure anyone would care.

Leaning in, he put his lips to my ear and snarled, "You're in my world now. Losing River is just the tip of how bad I could fuck you. You think Manuel is rotting in a prison cell because he cooperated? Don't fucking test me, Cora. This is not a fight a woman like you wants to take on."

The pressure in my chest mounted as the adrenaline and the lack of oxygen made my head light. "What...do...you want?" I choked out.

I waited for him to once again ask me where Catalina was.

I waited for him to hit me or scream at me.

I waited for him to strangle me until I passed out or died when I told him that I didn't know where she was.

But I never, not in a million years, expected his next words.

"Tell her to stay gone," he seethed. "I swear to God, she

gets one fucking idea about showing back up here to claim her brothers' estates, thinking she can waltz back in, ruin my career because now she has a dime in her pocket... Fuck her. I will kill both of you before I let that happen."

My vision was tunneling and my lungs were screaming for oxygen, but my mind couldn't process his words. It was like he was speaking a different language.

Thomas had spent years trying to find Catalina. The same way the Guerreros thought they owned me, Thomas believed with his whole heart that he owned her. Manuel had all but given her to him as a gift. In his eyes, she was the lucky one. No one walked away from a man like Thomas Lyons. Add to the fact that she'd taken his daughter with her... Forget about it. I'd always imagined he'd be still trying to find her on his deathbed to make her pay. But now he wanted her to stay gone?

"I don't..." *Understand.* "know where she—"

He gave me a hard shake, slamming me into the wall, knocking what little air I had left from my chest. Closing in on me, he pressed his large frame against my side. "Don't you fucking lie to me. You know where she is. You have *always* known. I was willing to let you keep your secret when it benefited me. But if Catalina thinks for one second that her piece-of-shit brothers being ash is her cue to come out of hiding, she obviously needs a reminder of who she really needs to fear."

I gasped for air when he slid his hand up to my jaw. His fingers bit into my face as he tilted my head up so I would look at him.

His malevolent gaze locked on mine as he seethed, "If

you ever want to see River again, you will pick up the fucking phone and tell that bitch to *stay...gone.*"

He released me with a shove, pain detonating in my head when it cracked against the wall. Whether it was because of my shaking legs, my blurred vision, or my heaving chest, my ability to balance on my own two feet disappeared. My only options were to eat the tile floor or sink to my ass.

I chose the latter but kept my eyes on Thomas as best I could.

He straightened his suit coat and ran a hand over the top of his hair to smooth it back into place. "I took the liberty of scheduling your hearing with Judge Mayso for next week. Before you get too excited, he owes me more favors than I have time. You get word to Catalina, I'll make sure everything is dropped and you get River back, no questions asked. But I'm watching you, Cora. I catch so much as a scent of that bitch in this city and you can kiss that child goodbye. Say you understand me."

With my heart in my throat, I nodded.

"Say it!" he demanded, rushing toward me.

I told my body not to flinch. I wanted to be strong enough to lock my emotions down the way I'd trained myself over the last decade. But in just one week, I'd become so emotionally raw that I couldn't fake it anymore. In that time, every emotion I'd ever possessed had gone to war inside me, my body physically becoming nothing more than the ravaged battlegrounds left behind.

It was supposed to be over.

I was supposed to be free.

But maybe freedom was nothing more than a delusion

to convince people like me to continue working in hell. Without the light at the end of the tunnel, we'd accept the darkness for what it truly was: eternal.

I closed my eyes, bracing for his assault, and rushed out, "I got it. I heard you. She won't come back. I promise."

"I hope for your sake you can keep your word on that."

I peeked up when I heard his footsteps moving away. The door opened silently, the sound of people in the distance being the only proof.

He paused before exiting. "You're free to go, Ms. Guerrero. Do take care of yourself."

Then he was gone.

And I was alone.

So. *Utterly*. Alone.

CHAPTER FIVE

Cora

I t was just before midnight when I walked out of the police station. Penn's truck was sitting out front and the sight of Drew climbing out of the driver's door equally felt like the sweetest relief and salt to a wound.

He was a friendly face.

And a liar.

But, sad as it was, he was also the only person I had left.

The tears finally breached my eyes as he jogged over and wrapped me into a tight hug that paled in comparison to his brother's.

"Are you okay?" he asked.

I shook my head. "Nope. Not even close."

Using my shoulders, he shifted me away from him. "What's going on? What are they charging you with?"

I swiped at the moisture dripping down my face. "Being a Guerrero." Starting toward the truck, I asked, "Did you bring my phone?"

He fell into step at my side. "Yeah. It's on the seat. Did you hear anything about River? Can we go pick her up?"

The rusty knife twisted inside me. "No. Social Services

has her until my court date next week."

"What the hell? You didn't do anything wrong. They can't charge you with child endangerment and not follow it up with proof."

"If you're Thomas Lyons, you can."

Drew came to a dead stop. "What did you say?"

I kept walking, too focused on calling Catalina to worry about his reaction.

After beelining straight to the passenger door, I leaned in to grab my phone. "I need a minute," I said, searching through my contacts for her number. I made it exactly one step before I face-planted against Drew's chest.

"Repeat it," he growled. "What did you say?"

I craned my head back, and the streetlight in the parking lot illuminated the fury etched in his face.

When his anger leveled on me, his eyes flared wide as he boomed, "And what the hell happened to your face?"

I rubbed my aching jaw. I could already feel the bruises from Thomas's fingertips forming on my face and neck—a not-so-subtle reminder that I had something to do.

"Move. I need to make a call."

He grabbed my arm, pulling me toward him. "No. Start talking. Did Thomas Lyons do that to you?"

"Yes!" I snapped, my voice echoing off cars parked on either side of us. "And if you don't get out of my way and let me make this call, he's going to do a lot worse." I snatched my arm out of his hold.

His eyes got dark, his lips got tight, and his lean body became murderous. "Get in the truck," he ordered on a low grumble.

"Get out of my—hey!" It wasn't rough nor was it gentle, but one second later, I found myself inside Penn's truck, the door slammed behind me, and Drew storming around the hood.

"He did not just manhandle me," I whispered to myself, the trauma of the day finally manifesting in violent rage.

He opened the door and climbed in, which was when I screamed at a decibel that should never be used in an enclosed vehicle. "You did not just manhandle me!"

"I sure as fuck did." He cranked the truck, threw it in reverse, and then hit the gas, all but peeling out of the parking spot.

"Are you kidding me right now?" I grabbed my seat belt and clicked it on. "Because clearly my day hasn't been bad enough—you need to go psychotic on me too?"

His jaw ticked as he jumped the curb to get on to the road. "What the fuck do you mean he's going to do a lot worse? Start at the beginning. I want to hear every goddamn detail that involves Thomas Lyons."

"Oh, suddenly, I'm supposed to be answering *your* questions now? When you've been lying to me for a fucking week?"

He tore his gaze off the road long enough to glance over at me. "The hell are you talking about? I haven't been lying to you."

"Bullshit!" I yelled, hooking my leg up on the seat so I could face him. "You've been lying to me about *everything* since the night of the fire. I don't know why. And I don't know what you're hiding. But don't you dare sit there and demand an explanation from me when you've never given one to me."

He sucked in a shaky breath as though he were searching for patience. "Has it ever occurred to you that maybe I'm trying to protect you?"

"Has it ever occurred to you that I don't want to be protected? I want the truth. I've spent my entire life being lied to, manipulated, and controlled, and now, you want me to just shut up and swallow more of it from you?"

He opened his mouth, but I didn't have time for any more bullshit explanations. They weren't going to contain anything but smoke and mirrors anyway.

"Save it, okay?" I picked my phone up again, but my mind was spinning in too many different directions to remember what I'd programmed Catalina's number under. Not like I could call her in front of Drew anyway.

Or did it even matter anymore?

I hadn't meant to explode on him, though I didn't exactly feel bad about it, either. Between Thomas's new shit, River being gone, my inability to find Savannah, the gaping hole in my heart because of Penn's death... I couldn't take much more. Everything on my body hurt—inside and out. I was beyond exhausted. And, worst of all, I missed the comfort of my hell in that apartment building. I just wanted to go home, where something—*anything*—felt normal again.

"I'm done, Drew. I'm so done."

"Don't say that." He sighed. "You don't understand."

"No. I really don't," I told the windshield. "Because you haven't given me a chance."

"Jesus Christ." He said it like a curse, but it was filled with resignation. "Didn't you and Penn used to play that game? Truth or Lies or something."

My throat got tight and I swung my head in his direction. "I don't want any more lies."

For a split second, headlights from oncoming traffic lit up the cab of the truck, enabling me to see his wince. "I need an out, Cora. Some of this shit, you do not need to know. And that is not because it's some great secret that will unlock the mysteries of the universe. It's because *I* don't want to know some of this shit. I'll give you what I can, but if there's something that you don't need to know, I'm not going to answer."

I chewed on the inside of my cheek. It wasn't ideal. But any light was better than staying in the dark. "Fine. Truth or Lie."

"All right. Lay it on me."

"Where'd he get a million dollars?"

"Lie. I don't know."

I shot him a glare. "Did he steal it? Rob a bank? What? The girls have it now. Are they going to get arrested for using it?"

"Truth. No. They'll be fine. Next question."

I rolled my eyes. "Okay, why'd he go to the building that night?"

He groaned and then lifted a pack of cigarettes into the air. "You mind if I smoke while we talk?"

I didn't care if he knitted a sweater while flying on the trapeze if he was actually going to tell me the truth.

"Go for it," I replied.

He rolled his window down before sparking the tip. Then he pulled in a few deep tobacco-filled inhales and blew them out of the truck. "He was pissed about what Dante did to Savannah, and he knew it wasn't going to stop at that. After everything he went through with Lisa, the idea of those ass-holes hurting you or River next... Well, it was more than he could take. I turned our cell phone records over to the cops. I didn't want to tell you because I thought it would only hurt you more, but he called Marcos and Dante that night. Couple times. I don't know what was said, but I can only imagine it was pretty colorful."

I screwed my eyes shut. Yeah, that hurt. Knowing that I was Penn's motive crashed into me like a sledgehammer.

Though finally having the truth made catching my breath a fraction easier.

"So he poked the beast and they actually showed up?" I asked.

"From what I've gathered, yeah, that's exactly what he did."

I spoke around the lump in my throat. "And he started the fire, didn't he? Was that his plan all along—to kill Marcos and Dante?"

He took another drag of his cigarette but never gave me his eyes. "Yes."

"And he did that for me too, didn't he?"

"Yeah."

It was a simple answer that needed no explanation.

I closed my eyes when they started to sting. I was so sick of crying all the damn time. "I knew it," I mumbled. "I fuck-ing knew it."

Drew's hand landed on the side of my neck, where he gave me a gentle squeeze. "The truth is, Cora, he loved you, and he was going to do whatever it took to make you safe."

"Yeah, well. If you want *my* truth, I'd rather them still be alive than him be dead."

"I know. But you gotta understand that I'm here, taking care of you, doing the best I can in a way that I know he would want. I'm on your team. And I'm sick of watching you cry, so if I can prevent that, sometimes, I might tell you a lie. But it's only to protect you. Not all lies are bad."

That little blast from the past made me stammer, "Y... you sound just like him. He used to tell me that too."

"Oh, come on, Penn isn't that smart."

I laughed, but it ended on a sob. "I miss him, Drew. So damn much. And I'm really mad at him. I didn't think I'd ever find someone after I lost Nic. And I don't even want to try after losing Penn. It's not worth it. In my life, nothing is permanent but pain. It's always one sprint after another. I haven't even caught my breath after losing Penn, and now, Thomas is trying to take River from me?"

The truck slowed to a stop on the shoulder of the road, but the dam inside me had broken. "What did I do wrong? I'm a good person, but I'm tired of being strong. I'm tired of fighting losing battles. And I'm tired of making the best out of a bad situation for the sake of everyone around me."

He put the truck in park and leaned toward me to give me some awkward side hug thing. "Shhh...calm down. Get it together, because we're gonna figure this out," he soothed.

But I couldn't get it together. My life had fallen apart the moment I first laid eyes on Nic Guerrero. And now, fourteen years later, there was nothing left of me but jagged remnants and broken shards. None of the pieces fit anymore, and I was too damn tired of trying to make them.

"I quit," I told his shoulder. "The universe can have its

victory, because I can't take this anymore."

"You're not a quitter. Or we wouldn't be sitting here right now."

I sat up, swiping at my eyes. "He took my daughter, Drew. And unless I can get in touch with Catalina and convince her *not* to come back to claim her brothers' estates, he says he'll take her away from me for good. And he's just sick and twisted enough that I believe him. Though I'm not sure if that's before or after he kills me. Something he also threatened. So maybe I should worry about that one first."

The day I'd met Drew Walker, I'd thought he was plain. But, in hindsight, that had only been because he was standing next to Penn.

Drew was a different kind of handsome.

A different kind of sweet.

A different kind of thoughtful.

And, right then, with his jaw tight, his eyes narrowed into slits, the muscles straining at his neck, and his lips forming a hard slash, he was kind of scary too.

"What?" he breathed so quietly that I barely heard him over the rumble of the engine.

"And he sent the attorney you found home tonight. Apparently, they play golf together. Annnnnnd…the judge that will be hearing my case owes him more favors than Thomas has time. How am I supposed to fight that? Because seriously, if you have an idea, I'm all ears. 'Cause I got nothing."

"Oh, I got a plan." He stared at me. His lips were curled into a rabid snarl and his chest was rising and falling faster with every breath, but his eyes weren't focused. It was as though he were looking right through me.

I waited for several seconds, but when he failed to offer an explanation, I prompted, "You care to share it with me?"

He blinked, turned in his seat, put the car back into gear, and hit the gas. "Nope."

I watched him closely as he weaved through traffic. He wasn't driving fast or overly aggressive, but the muscles in his arms flexed like he was trying to rip the wheel off the steering column.

By the time he opened the door to our hotel room, he'd relaxed a good bit. I, on the other hand, was a mess. One look around that empty room and I wanted to fall apart all over again. Thanks to the Guerreros, I had missed years of River growing up. But ever since Manuel had gotten locked away, she hadn't spent a single night away from me.

Now, I didn't even know where she was.

Her clothes were strewn haphazardly in what was supposed to be a pile in the corner, and her phone was still charging on the nightstand.

Never had my chest felt emptier.

But crying wasn't going to get my daughter back.

Drew was right: I wasn't a quitter, no matter how appealing the idea sounded sometimes.

I had no doubt River would call me the first chance she got. She was smart, and as much as I'd hated all the shit she'd had to deal with in her thirteen years, it gave me comfort that she knew how to handle herself in any situation.

I had a week before the court date. I needed to get in touch with Catalina and figure out our next move. I couldn't live like that. I'd just gotten rid of two problems without adding Thomas Lyons to my list. Even if that meant finding River and taking off the same way Catalina had done all those years earlier. Once I got the rest of the girls from the building taken care of, I didn't have much of a reason to stay anymore.

The building was gone.

Penn too.

And, while I did care about Drew, it wasn't like he was going to spend the rest of his life beside me on the bed. Nor did I want him to. However, I was weak enough to let him stay until I got River back.

But what would happen after that? I'd always be looking over my shoulder. Holding my breath. Waiting for the day Thomas or one of his henchmen in blue found us.

It hadn't even been two weeks since Marcos and Dante died. But there was something inherently addictive about not having to monitor your every move.

I didn't think before I spoke.

I cried without fear of it being used against me.

And I didn't wake up four times a night to make sure the doors were locked.

Penn had given up his life to make me free. Thomas didn't get to take that away.

But what other choice did I have?

"I need to make a call," I told Drew as I started scrolling through my phone.

He sat across from me on the bed. "Catalina?"

My gaze jumped to his. I could have lied. I could have protected her. I could have kept up the façade that I was just as clueless as everyone else when it came to where she had gone. But damn, I was tired of hiding.

"Yeah," I whispered. "Please don't ask any questions."

He gave my knee a reassuring squeeze. "How about I head down to the hotel bar for a little while. Give you some time alone. You can call me if you need anything though. Okay?"

I nodded. "Thanks, Drew."

"Any time, Cora. Any time."

I stared at my phone until the door clicked behind him. After that, I scrolled through until I found the number I'd programmed in as Delilah's Bakery and hit call.

She answered on the first ring.

"I need you to come back, Cat."

"Have you lost your freaking mind?"

"No. I've lost my daughter."

The line went silent—along with my heart.

CHAPTER SIX

Penn

"Please, Penn!" Cora screamed.

I'd climbed out of her window and was staring up at the flames, which if everything were going as planned, were finishing off Marcos and Dante forever.

But she wasn't supposed to be there.

She was supposed to be at the hotel.

She was...

As she banged on the windowpanes, her blue eyes filled with terror, fire licking at her back, smoke all around her. "Please, Penn!" Her voice tore through me with the velocity of a bullet, knocking the wind out of my lungs before piercing through my heart.

"Cora!" I yelled, lurching toward the building, ready to claw my way up to her, but my legs wouldn't move any more than her name carried any sound.

I couldn't move.

I couldn't breathe.

All I could do was watch her die.

Such was my curse in life.

I came awake with a loud roar shredding my throat.

Bolting upright, I panted and frantically tried to differentiate my nightmare from reality.

It wasn't the first nightmare I'd had about her. She was my subconscious's favorite obsession as of late.

She was always dying.

I was always watching.

And I could never get to her.

With a shaking hand, I scrubbed my face, desperately trying to wipe away the mental image of her standing at that window. In the dark, I patted the bed beside me as if she would suddenly appear.

What I would have given for her to be there with me, physically reassuring me while my mind took the longer path to keep up.

My pulse slowed as I closed my eyes and imagined her there.

She would have purred as I rolled her over, stretching like a cat before circling her arms around my neck. Her heart beating. Air in her lungs. Safe at my side.

Her messy, blond hair would have cascaded over her face, barely revealing a sleepy smile as she murmured, "You 'kay, baby?"

When I would have told her no, that I needed her, her eyes would have opened, the blue sparkling even in the darkness, healing me as she whispered, "I'm right here, Penn."

And then she would have kissed me, slow and soft, with a reverence that made it seem like maybe I was healing her too.

As it always did with us, it wouldn't have taken long before it became heated. Her hands roaming over my back, and as mine drifted to her ass, the nightmare would fade as desire overwhelmed us both.

She would have opened her legs, inviting me in.

And I would have slid in, more desperate than ever to bury myself inside her warmth.

Alone, in my bedroom, I could almost feel her fingertips gliding over my shoulder as our bodies rolled together, and as I fell back against the pillows, the sound of her moans playing in my ears, I absolutely felt my hand slide into my sweats and wrap around my thickening cock.

"Fucking hell. What are you doing?" a man growled.

My entire body came awake for a second time as I flew out of bed, the gun under my pillow coming up with me, my finger poised.

"Whoa, whoa, whoa! It's me! Shane, stop!" he yelled.

The jarring familiarity was the only thing that stopped me from pulling the trigger, but I still couldn't process who he was or why he was there.

"Who the fuck are you!" I boomed, lifting the gun higher, stepping toward his indistinguishable silhouette.

"It's me. Drew. Shit, man. It's me! Put the gun down!"

My breath left me on a rush. "Jesus, Drew! What the hell are you doing here? Don't sneak up on a man like that."

He slapped on the light, nearly blinding me. "I didn't sneak up on you, dickhead. I woke your sorry ass up. You sat up and everything. Then you went for your dick like the start of some seriously fucked-up porn."

Okay, so I clearly had not fully woken up between my nightmare-turned-wet-dream.

Well played, subconscious. Well played.

Using one arm to shield my eyes from the light, I opened the drawer on my nightstand and tucked the gun inside. "You scared the shit out of me."

He planted his hands on his hips. "Yeah, well. I'd way rather that any day over watching you jerk your dick."

"Would you shut the fuck up?" I hissed.

And then, as if on cue…

"Penn?" Her frightened voice fluttered down the hallway.

Outstanding.

I started toward the door to put her mind at ease when I caught a glimpse of Drew's face. Swear to God, his mouth was hanging open so wide that I thought his jaw was going to come unhinged.

"Are you fucking kidding me right now?" he snarled. "It hasn't even been two weeks and you got a woman here? Are. You. *Kidding* me?"

I shot him a bored glare. "It's Savannah, you ass."

When I got into the hall, I found her standing outside her bedroom door. She was still wearing the oversized sleep shirt, but she'd shed the pajama pants at some point.

"Go back to bed. It's just Drew," I told her.

"Is everything okay?" she asked.

I uncomfortably scratched the back of my head. "Yeah. He…surprised me. That's all."

She visibly relaxed until Drew took the opportunity to make things weird again.

"Oh my God, please tell me you're not seriously sleeping with Savannah."

I jerked around, ready to feed him my fist just to make him shut the hell up, but Savannah got there first.

"Ew! No! That'd be gross. Penn's my new daddy."

My life, ladies and gentlemen. My life.

I snapped my fingers at Savannah. "Stop saying that." Then I looked back at Drew. "And you, stop saying *anything*. I woke up, like, thirty-seven seconds ago. Can I please have a minute to figure what day of the week it is before dealing with your ludicrous accusations?"

With a challenge, he stepped toward me. "It's Thursday. Now, what the hell is she doing here?"

Stealing a move from Cora's playbook, I rolled my eyes, walked past him, and headed straight to the coffee maker, calling out, "Go back to bed, kid."

"Night, Drew. Night—"

"Don't say it, Savannah," I grumbled, cutting her off before whatever variation of dad fell from her tongue.

She giggled, but thankfully, only Drew's footsteps followed after me.

I gave him my back as I went to work on the coffee grounds. I'd texted Drew the address from my new phone as soon as I'd secured the place. Though I'd never given him a key or the security code.

"How'd you get in?" I asked, taking out two mugs.

"Why is she here?" he replied.

I'd have rather gone back to listening to him talk about my dick than have this conversation. But there was no way he was going to let it go. "I promised Cora I'd get her back."

"Yeah," he scoffed. "Then you *died*."

I turned around, propping my ass against the counter. "No, Drew. Penn Walker died. But me, Shane? I promised Cora that day that I'd get her back. So I did."

His mouth gaped as he gave me a slow blink. "And what now? You just gonna keep the kid forever? Because she sure as hell can't go back to Cora now."

I crossed my arms over my chest. "And why not?"

"Because you are *dead!*" He started pacing the length of the kitchen. "What the hell is going through your head right now? First, you leave her all those damn stars and the money, and then you blow everything to get the kid?"

"I didn't blow anything. What would you have rather me do? Leave her there? She was standing on a freaking street corner, looking for a john so she could buy drugs."

He stopped pacing, raking a rough hand through the top of his hair. "You could have called *me*. I would have gone and gotten her."

"I didn't have time for that," I stated definitively.

He rubbed his eyes with his thumb and forefinger. "You didn't have time? Or didn't want to make time? Because I'll be honest: I think you're doing this shit on purpose. You shut the door with Cora, but you've been leaving the window cracked every chance you get. You planning to come back, *Penn*? Something I need to know about?"

"That's not what I'm doing."

"Then open your damn mouth and tell me what you *are* doing. Giving money to the poor? Saving kids off the street? Coming back from the grave? Where I'm standing, it looks like you're one step away from becoming Jesus Christ himself."

"I'm not coming back!"

He leveled me with a glare. "But you're not ruling it out, either, are you?"

I didn't have an answer to that.

Yes, leaving her was safer.

Yes, it'd destroyed me.

Yes, I'd spent every minute since the fire imagining getting her back.

Without question, I was going after Thomas Lyons, and there were only three scenarios for how that would end.

More than likely, I'd get caught and sentenced to life in prison. And if that were the case, I didn't want her life stopping with mine. Knowing Cora, she'd have baked cakes with nail files in them for the rest of her life. She was stubborn as hell, and God knew I wasn't strong enough to ever shake her off. But I wanted more than that for her. I wanted her to make a life. A real one.

The idea of her being with any other man was enough to send me off the edge of a bridge. He'd never be good enough. But I smiled at the thought of her having a family, a bunch of little blond girls who could call her mom without fear of retaliation. This was the scenario that had convinced me to leave her the cash.

The other possible outcome for me was that I'd fail. Thomas would somehow kill me or get me locked away first. Cora was already on his radar because of Catalina, but the last thing she needed was to be connected to me in any way, shape, or form. She'd become his next target and I'd be six feet under, helpless to save her. This was the scenario that had made it so obvious that Penn Walker needed to die. Without him, there was nothing connecting Shane Pennington and Cora Guerrero. If I failed, she had money. She had Drew. She had a safety net.

However, it was that last possible outcome that played in my head every night when I stared up at the starless ceiling. It was the one where I'd killed him and gotten away with it. The world would be a better place, and I'd walk away free and clear. The chances of that happening were almost zilch. You couldn't take out the city's DA and expect to ride off into the sunset. But it was the one scenario that gave me hope of getting her back, and no matter how hard I'd tried, I couldn't let it go.

I didn't want to admit it. But it was that last scenario that was fueling me day in and day out.

And as I'd learned the day I'd choked the life out of Dante while his terrified brother watched, knowing he was next: There wasn't much I wouldn't do for Cora Guerrero.

Turning back to the gurgling coffee pot, I poured a mug as I declared, "I'm not talking about this anymore. When Thomas takes his last breath, then we can worry about what I'm going to do or not do next."

"Right, well. I guess I should tell you that, if you're hoping Cora lives long enough to be part of that equation, you might want to hurry up on the whole making-Thomas-stop-breathing thing."

Fire hit my veins. "What the fuck does that mean?"

He arrogantly tipped his head. "You heard me. Thomas made a little appearance tonight. Trumped up some child endangerment charge against Cora, had her arrested, and took River."

Another blast of adrenaline hit me hard. "What the fuck? Where the hell were you?"

He narrowed his eyes. "Lying in the bed next to her. I

can't fight the cops, Shane. That's how a man gets dead. Fast. I got her an attorney, but Thomas sent him home. They play golf or some shit. He cornered Cora though. Told her to make sure Catalina stays gone or they're both dead." His mouth kept moving, but no words made it past the sound of my heart roaring in my ears.

Visions of Lisa lying on that carpet exploded in my head. Only this time, Cora was beside her. Both sets of their cold, dead eyes staring back at me.

Before I knew it, I had my fists wrapped in the front of Drew's shirt, my face vibrating as I ordered, "He does not *ever* come near her again. Do you understand me?"

He gave me a hard shove, but my body was so amped my every muscle was screaming. He might as well have been pushing a brick wall.

"That's why I'm here, asshole. You gotta speed this shit up. Get off your ass, quit playing Nanny McGee, and handle this once and for all. Or get out of my way and let me take care of it on my own."

I stared at him with wild eyes. "He's mine."

"Then consider this your courtesy heads-up. I'm not feeling real patient anymore. He's been breathing for four fucking years, Shane. You want your twenty-nine minutes. Take 'em. But if I get a clear shot before then, it's over. You got me?"

"That was not the plan, Drew."

"What plan?" He swung a hand out and pointed down the hall to Savannah's bedroom. "You have shit all over every fucking plan we've ever made. Currently, we got a woman who has you tied up in so many damn knots you're unrecognizable anymore. I thought she was good for you at first, but now, she's got you so off-kilter you can't even think straight." He sucked in a deep breath and gripped my shoulder, giving it a rough squeeze. "I know you've been dreaming about this. And I know I promised you that you could have your moment with him. For Lisa. But, brother, this shit's gotta end. We found him. Now, let's *finish him.*"

He was so right.

It had been four years.

Four years of searching for answers.

Four years of bleeding myself dry emotionally and physically.

Four years of burning in the flames of hell.

Those two months spent drowning in Cora, feeling like myself again, thinking more than minute to minute were the only reason I was still able to function.

There was nothing I wouldn't do to get back to that.

Not even sacrificing the very same revenge that had brought me to her door.

I extended a hand his way. "I want Cora to be priority one. You have a shot. You take it. As long as we can keep her out of his reach. I'll deal."

He grinned, taking my hand. "Now, that actually sounds like a plan we can make stick." He pulled me in for a quick back pat, and before he released me, he did what Drew did best: He made me want to laugh and then feed him my fist again. "I can't believe you were trying to get me to watch you jerk your dick. You know I don't swing like that."

I barked a laugh and gave him a hard push. "Get the fuck out of my apartment."

He backed away with his arms spread wide. "Nice place, by the way."

"You still staying at the hotel with her?"

"Yep." He rubbed his hands together. "Saving up my rewards points for a nice little vacation when this is finally over. I'm thinking Brazil. Topless beaches and all."

"A job will get you there faster."

He twisted his lips. "Psshh, who needs a job when you got a rich best friend who owes you for saving his future wife's ass a time or seven hundred?"

A few months back, hearing him say something like that would have sent me into a tailspin. Now though? It gave me hope that maybe walking out of this with her wasn't as impossible as I'd once thought.

"How's she doing?"

His smile fell. "You want truth or lie?"

Truth or lie. Those simple words made pain detonate in my chest. Christ, he really had been hanging out with her. And damn, it made me jealous.

"Truth."

He shook his head. "Not good. Not good at all. She knows I'm lying about the fire. I dribbled her some stuff tonight and I think it made her feel better. But she misses you and blames herself."

"Shit," I breathed, pinching the bridge of my nose while guilt rotted my gut.

"But we're gonna fix this. Thomas first. Then we can worry about the full-body cast that woman is going to put you in for faking your own death." He winked.

CHAPTER SEVEN

Cora

The morning after I was released, I got a call from a social worker asking if she could swing by the hotel and pick up River's things. After the fire, the kid didn't own much, so I went to the mall and picked up a few things I'd thought she would like. She'd probably hate them all. But it made me feel better. The social worker also informed me that she was allowed to have her phone. I nearly burst into tears at that news. They wouldn't let me see her, but at least we'd been able to talk.

River called me each night and I could tell by the tone of her voice it was because she missed me.

But in the mornings, I knew she only called because she was worried about me.

It was no secret that mornings were hard for me. That first blink when I'd slip from blissful lala land into consciousness, remembering where I was as an avalanche of hellish memories hit me like they were happening the very first time.

Day after day, every time the sun rose, that moment of realization was agony.

But if I wanted to get my daughter back, I couldn't

wallow in self-pity. I had to get up and make things happen.

River was not wrong. Seven hundred and fifty dollars didn't get you much when it came to housing in the city. Though, on the outskirts, it got me a two-bedroom quasi-piece-of-shit house that included water.

Drew and I were picking up the keys late that afternoon when I got a call from the group home letting me know the case against me had been dropped and I could come get River anytime I would like. I shrieked and my new landlord looked at me like he was already regretting his decision to give me the house. I could not have cared less how crazy he thought I was though. My girl was coming home.

And then we were getting out of that life for good.

I couldn't decide what Thomas was playing at. My court date wasn't for another few days and I'd figured he'd drag it out as long as the law would allow.

But whatever the reason, if it got me River back, I wasn't going to complain.

As Drew pulled into the parking lot, I spotted Thomas's Cadillac. Dread filled my stomach, but with the countdown on, his reign of corruption was nearing an end.

I froze halfway out. "What are you doing?"

Drew also stilled, his door open, one of his boots on the asphalt. He quirked an eyebrow. "Going with you?"

"No. You're staying here."

"You've lost your damn mind, woman."

"You walk in there with me, he's going to assume you're my boyfriend. I'm not handing him one more person to use against me next time he gets pissed."

"He can assume whatever the fuck he wants, but he gets

the wild hair to put his hands on you again and I'm gonna be there to lock that shit down real quick."

And that was *exactly* why I couldn't let Drew come inside with me.

Over the last week, I'd learned that, while in jail, Manuel had filled Drew in on all things Thomas Lyons. It didn't surprise me in the least that even four years later, Manuel was still fuming. He firmly believed that no one crossed a Guerrero. And Thomas had not only turned on him, but he'd used Manuel's own daughter to put him away—the ultimate stab in the back.

It also didn't surprise me that Drew had spent the last week ranting and raving about Thomas. He hadn't been able to look at me without getting pissed over the bruises on my face and neck. I couldn't imagine what would have happened if they came face-to-face. Thomas's monstrosity of an ego would never allow that confrontation to end in Drew's favor.

"He's not going to pull anything," I assured him. "It's a group home for teens. I won't be the only one in there. He'll be on his best pretentious-lawyer behavior. Come on, Drew. He got the charges dropped. Don't give him another reason to stir up more trouble for us."

"They were bullshit charges to begin with. He's hardly a hero."

"No. But I'm getting River back. Let's try not to make any waves today." I climbed the rest of the way out of the truck, facing him as I straightened my mint green tank-top and smoothed my wind-tousled hair down. "What about this…" I retrieved my phone and punched in his number. A muffled ringing came from his back pocket. "You can listen. If you hear anything that doesn't seem right, you're only a few yards away."

He closed his eyes, shaking his head. "Penn would literally body-slam me for even considering this."

Some days were easier than others. Sometimes the thought of Penn slashed through me like shrapnel. Other times, the memory of him gave me peace and comfort. And that day, as I was only minutes away from getting my daughter back, I actually smiled at the thought of Penn's angry scowl.

"Please, Drew."

He retrieved the phone and answered by putting it to his ear and saying, "This line disconnects and I'm busting through that door like the Kool-Aid man."

I giggled.

He glowered—definitely related to Penn.

But before he had the chance to change his mind, I said, "I'll be right back," and shut the door.

Holding my phone, I jogged up the sidewalk to the front door and then knocked.

A woman in her late forties with a severe case of resting bitch face answered. "Can I help you?"

I smiled wide and genuine. "I'm here to pick up my daughter."

Her nose crinkled as she gave me a confused head-to-toe. It was everyone's reaction when they found out I had a teenage daughter. I'd always looked younger than I was, which at twenty-nine was a blessing when it came to forking out cash on anti-wrinkle serum, but not so much when it came to convincing people I was a fit mother.

"River," I filled in when she didn't reply. "Guerrero."

Her eyebrows shot up, but it didn't soften her judgmental glare.

Thomas's large frame appeared behind her. His lips tipped up in a slimy grin as he met my gaze, his words aimed at the woman. "Cynthia, I'll handle this. Get the child."

"Sure. No problem," she said, strolling away with the speed of a slug.

My pulse quickened and I clutched the phone tighter, careful not to press any of the buttons.

"Cora," he greeted, shoving a hand into the pocket of his slacks. "Do come in."

"Thanks," I whispered, stepping over the threshold.

He glanced over his shoulder in time to see Ms. Cheery exit through a door leading deeper into the building. "I trust you've been in touch with Catalina."

I shifted my gaze to the wall and used my free hand to worry my necklace. "She won't be back."

He arched a dark eyebrow. "And what happens if that changes?"

"I'll lose River forever," I answered robotically.

He lowered his voice and stepped forward, crowding me. "Or?"

I swallowed hard, but it was purely for show. I wasn't scared of Thomas anymore. "Or you'll kill me."

He traced a finger around the curve of my face, dipping under my chin to tip my head back. "How is my daughter, Cora? She's, what...fourteen now?"

I didn't reply. He didn't deserve to know anything about Isabel.

The day he married Catalina, it was nothing more than a deal brokered by Manuel. He made the corrupt attorney with dreams of becoming a judge a part of the family. And Thomas got a beautiful wife to stand at his side, her father's money backing him, and one of the city's biggest criminals in his back pocket feeding him the competition like shark bait.

Isabel hadn't been planned. Two people usually needed to be having sex to plan something like that. But one night after Thomas had come home drunk declaring that it was his wife's duty to open her legs to him, everything changed. She was already pregnant when I'd met Nic. But the family knew what was happening between him and Catalina. Nic and Dante had gone to blows over it.

But Manuel had needed Thomas, so he'd turned a blind eye and his daughter later sold him down the river for it.

"She won't be back," I repeated. "I swear to you. They won't cause you any problems."

Playing up the fear, I allowed my breath to hitch as he leaned in close.

His face was mere inches from mine, his breath whispering across my skin as he said, "That's good to hear. But do not get comfortable, Cora. I don't waste my time with idle threats. You cross me and you're done. It wouldn't be a bad idea to pass that message along to my wife as well."

"Of course. I'll remind her."

He grinned, and then in time with the creak of a door behind us, he abruptly stepped away.

"Cora," River called, jogging over and throwing her arms around my neck.

I kept my eyes on Thomas as I pulled her into a hug.

"Hey, baby."

"Here's your things," the woman said, shuffling over with a grocery sack dangling from the tip of her finger, her phone charger hanging out of a hole in the bottom. She turned a scowl on me. "Maybe next time you should get her an actual *bag*."

"There won't be a next time," I stated as absolute fact.

"Then we're clear?" he pressed.

"Crystal," I murmured.

"Don't forget your phone." He grabbed River's cell off the corner of the woman's desk and offered it her way.

If looks could kill, River would have saved us all a lot of trouble right then and there.

"Thanks," she muttered, snatching it from his hand.

After I threw my arm around her shoulders, we started toward the door together. While I wasn't buying into Thomas's all-powerful *Godfather* routine, I was more than ready to get the hell out of there.

"Oh, and, Cora," he called.

I curled River into my front as I put my chin to my shoulder to look at him. "Yeah?"

"Do say hello to Drew for me. It's a shame I wasn't able to meet him today, especially after hearing about what happened to his sister."

I blinked, and for the first time since I'd entered that room, I felt a sick sense of unease wash over me. I wasn't sure what he was talking about. Penn had point-blank told me that Drew was his only sibling. But it was the wicked smirk like he'd just dropped a bomb on me that set my teeth on edge. With chills prickling my skin, I opted not to stand around and ask questions.

I dipped my head in acknowledgement and then hurried out the door.

Drew was already out of the truck, sprinting toward us, his face dark and thunderous. "Are you okay?"

"I'm fine. Just get in the truck."

His jaw ticked as he stared at the building.

"Drew," I hissed, giving his arm a sharp tug. "Let's go."

"Right," he growled, reluctantly following after me.

After we were all in the truck and safely on the road, I turned to Drew. "Do you have a sister?"

He shook his head and white-knuckled the steering wheel. "He had to have been talking about Penn's wife."

I guessed that would have been his sister-in-law. "How does he know about that?"

"I don't know. But the fact that he knows who I am and that he's been digging around in my past doesn't sit right with me."

It didn't sit right with me, either, but by this time the next day, we wouldn't have to worry about it anymore.

"Drive around for a little while." I turned in my seat and looked out the back window. "Make sure we're not being followed."

His eyebrows drew together. "I thought you gave the social worker the new address yesterday?"

"I did. But we're not going home tonight." I reached into the back seat and took River's hand. "We're going to Catalina's."

Drew's head swung in my direction so fast that it was a wonder it didn't fly off his neck. "What!"

River gasped, stretching her seat belt to the limit as she lurched forward. "Is she back?"

I smiled; my girl did love her aunt. "Yeah. I fronted her some money to get a house a few days ago. With Marcos and Dante gone, she doesn't have to hide anymore."

Her big, doe eyes flared. "What about Thomas?"

"Yeah. What about Thomas?" Drew parroted, flicking his furious gaze between me and the road.

"Relax," I told them both.

"He took me away for funsies. Don't you think he'll do the same to Isabel?" River asked, her anxiety making an all-too-frequent appearance.

I gave her hand a squeeze. "He might try. But he won't be a problem after tomorrow. Catalina's going to the police. And before you say it, yes, I know firsthand how many crooked people he has at his disposal all across the city. But Catalina has been a missing person for years. Her sudden return will draw national attention the same way it did when she disappeared. Thomas doesn't have that kind of reach. Besides, she has more than enough on him to put him away forever. Thomas is an idiot. I never would have thought about it if he hadn't panicked and arrested me. Dante and Marcos didn't exactly have wills, and since Manuel is still in jail, Cat's the only Guerrero left. She'll inherit everything, River. *Everything.* The legit businesses. The property. The houses. All the stuff Manuel was forced to sign away to his sons when Thomas went after him."

"Great, so she has money now," Drew deadpanned. "That doesn't give her invincibility."

"No. But it makes *him* vulnerable. She's not stuck

anymore. Whether you want to admit it or not, money *is* power for people like us. No, it won't fix our problems, but it does give us room to breathe and a safety net to fall back on. Catalina walked away the first time with her pride and two hundred dollars. Best decision she ever made. But, now, she doesn't have to worry about how she's going to put food on the table. Or pay for a doctor when Isabel gets sick. Or buy school supplies or clothes or put gas in the car. Money doesn't equal security, but it does offer opportunity. This is our chance, Drew. Me and Cat. We've been dreaming of getting out of this life once and for all. And thanks to Penn, now that Marcos and Dante are out of the way, there's only one obstacle left." I rested my hand on his forearm. "I'm done hiding. I'm done letting the world roll over me. I'm done being a Guerrero. I want out. I can taste it. It's so close."

"Jesus, Cora," Drew breathed. "You think a man like that is just gonna let Catalina strut back in after four years without consequences?"

"There's not much he can do to her anymore. He's aching to get a spot on the bench. And with elections coming in a few months, he needs to start his campaign. Imagine how it's going to look when his wife and child pop back up, stating that they endured countless years of mental and physical abuse at his hands. Not to mention all the information Catalina has about his extracurricular activities. He fronts like he's a man of the law, but really, he's the puppet master behind at least half the crimes that happen in the city everyday. If she can get someone to listen, the proof is already there in the court records. Someone just needs to know *where* to look."

"He could kill her!" Drew exclaimed, his sudden

outburst causing River to flinch. "And *you* in the process. I'm sorry, but this is a stupid idea. That man is fucking dangerous, Cora. And I'm not talking about him trying to take River or whatever other bullshit he has up his sleeve. He has connections far worse than judges and Polo-wearing attorneys he plays golf with on the weekends. I'm talking about bad men who are trying to avoid being prosecuted. *Desperate men* who will literally do anything to stay on his good side. Finding someone to plow over you and Catalina will be a walk in the park."

I hooked my leg up onto the seat and turned to face him. "Wow. I'm truly touched by your confidence."

"This isn't a pep talk. This is the *truth*. That's what you said you wanted from me, right? No more lies? Fine. Then this is insane. And I want no part of it."

"Then walk away. No one is asking you to stay with us."

He barked a loud, humorless laugh. "If only that were true."

I narrowed my eyes on him. "What's that supposed to mean?"

He shook his head. "It doesn't fucking matter. You're going to do this shit whether I go with you or not, aren't you?"

I crossed my arms over my chest. "Yep."

Through clenched teeth, he gritted out, "Then I guess we're going to see the infamous Catalina Lyons today."

A victorious grin split my mouth.

He must have caught it out of the corner of his eye, because without looking at me, he bit out, "Wipe that smile off your face. I'm not happy about this." But he said it as he turned down a side street that was not on our way home. And as he started our hour-long detour through random neighborhoods, his gaze constantly flicking to the rearview mirror, he muttered, "Christ. Another fucking Nancy Drew. And he says he doesn't have a type."

CHAPTER EIGHT

Penn

Drew: Please tell me you have eyes on Thomas.
Me: On him now. Why?

I was sitting up the street from Thomas's house. It had become my nightly routine. With the parade of women, maids, colleagues, and a few randoms I'd yet to identify in and out of his house all week, it was proving more difficult than I'd ever thought to get the piece of shit alone. But tonight was the night.

He was with the brunette from the courthouse again. It marked the third time this week. And if it went anything like those nights, she'd tiptoe out around two in the morning, twisting only the lock on the knob before hurrying to her car. That gave me a full five hours before his maid showed up.

Pad that window with time to get in and out and I had four glorious hours to watch him die.

It was almost eleven. I pulled the security app up on my phone. And according to the camera above my front door, which I'd yet to mention to Savannah, she either was already in bed or had turned into Spider-Man, scaled down six floors, and gone out for the night. I was betting on the former. She'd been doing really well. I hadn't been able to get her into a real rehab facility yet, but I'd hired a private doctor who specialized in addiction who came by every couple of days, and I'd even gone to a few NA meetings with her too.

If I didn't make it back, I was really going to miss that kid. But she knew how to find Drew if anything ever happened to me. And since my will left everything to Cora Guerrero, I had peace of mind that they'd always be taken care of.

I stared at Drew's text as if I could read between the lines and find an explanation.

Me: You going to elaborate?

Ten minutes later, my chest was starting to get tight. He'd texted me earlier that day that they were going to pick up River. I'd hoped that meant Thomas was backing off Cora. But now…something didn't feel right.

Me: Hello! Is everything okay?

When another ten minutes passed without a response, my anxiety climbing with every tick of the second hand, I gave up on the waiting game and called.

It went to voicemail after the second ring.

Motion at Thomas's front door caught my attention. He was walking out with his hand on the brunette's lower back. He paused to lock up and then escorted her down the short walk to her silver Lexus.

The phone vibrated in my hand.

Drew: With Cora. Can't talk. Just stay on him until I can fill you in.

He was with her. I blew out a relieved breath. That was good. Really good, and my pulse responded immediately.

Brake lights backing out of Thomas's driveway drew my gaze up.

"Where do you think you're going?" I whispered as Thomas's Cadillac followed her Lexus out onto the main road.

I put my car in drive and eased out in the opposite direction. I'd hit the neighborhood loop and meet him at the entrance. But my suspicions grew as she turned left and he cut right. Okay, so they weren't going somewhere together. Not a huge deal, except Thomas wasn't known to be a night owl.

I followed him a few car lengths back as he drove across town. With the city lights twinkling behind us, he led me into the burbs. It was a nice-ish area. The houses were spread out and off the main road. The lack of traffic made it difficult to stay close. In his richy-rich neighborhood, my Audi blended right in. But there, I might as well have had a neon sign on my hood.

As he rolled to a stop, I quickly zipped into a nearby driveway and cut my lights, praying that the family who lived inside was fast asleep and not peering out the window. I sank low in my seat when a beat-up '90s-model sedan pulled up behind him. Two men climbed out and Thomas joined them, but he didn't greet them before taking off with long and heavy strides down the dark road, the newest additions to our party falling into step behind him.

"What the fuck are you doing?" I asked the night as I silently folded out of my car. I tucked my gun into the back of my jeans and skulked into the shadows.

Just when I was convinced Thomas was only out for some late-night cardio, the three men turned toward a quaint little brick house complete with a farmhouse mailbox. The street was dead that time of night, only a few porch lights exposing the homes.

But the front door he was heading toward had glowing windows wrapping all the way around. I inched closer, sinking deep into the wooded tree line that divided the homes.

And that's when everything stopped.

My heart.

The Earth.

Time.

My truck was sitting in the driveway.

My truck that I'd sold to Drew for a dollar.

My truck that I'd left Cora over a million dollars inside.

My fucking truck that Drew was no doubt driving that night.

And he was with Cora.

Panic iced my veins, stealing the air from my lungs. But one beat later, the rolling fire of adrenaline set me ablaze.

"Oh, shit," I breathed as Thomas walked straight to the front door, the two men splitting off in opposite directions, heading around to the back. I frantically weighed my options: I could go after Thomas or follow the two men who were entirely too reminiscent of the ones Thomas had sent to kill Lisa.

And then, somehow, everything got worse.

The front door yanked open and Thomas whipped a gun out of his pocket. I was barely able to make out the "Where the fuck is my wife?" before the gunshot exploded into the silent night.

I didn't think.

I didn't plan.

I didn't even consciously decide to move.

I just took off at a dead sprint, her blue eyes fueling my every step.

It took me a thousand years to reach that house. I darted up the driveway and then through the open door. As soon as my feet hit that fucking carpet, I scanned the room, searching for the only thing that could ever slow my racing heart.

She wasn't there. At least not that I could see.

Drew was sitting on Thomas's chest, his fist flying at his face. He paused long enough to turn his rabid gaze on mine, the flicker of recognition hitting him just before he continued his assault. "They're in the bedroom," he barked. "Go. Now."

My vision flashed red and my body graced me with yet another surge of power when the sound of a woman's gurgled scream echoed through the room.

"Cora!" I roared, following the commotion into the hall.

My lungs seized as I found one of Thomas's men straddling a woman. She kicked and flailed beneath him as he squeezed at her throat.

It wasn't Cora, but that only meant I still had no idea where she was.

Diving forward, I bulldozed him off her. The guy wasn't small by any standards, but he was clumsy and clearly not driven by raw emotion the way I was. We rolled together, banging against the walls until we reached one of the open bedrooms. We exchanged punches—however, with an endless source of rage feeding my fight, he soon fell limp.

I rose off his unconscious body and turned my prowl onto the woman who I recognized from pictures to be Catalina. Her brown eyes and smooth olive skin matched her brothers'.

"Where is she?" I rumbled, wiping the blood off my bottom lip with the back of my hand.

With tears streaming down her face, she lifted her hands in surrender. "W...wait," she stammered, backing into the corner.

"Cora. Tell me where she is," I demanded.

Coughing between words, she managed to choke out, "There's...nobody else...here. I swear. Nobody." Her whole body trembled as I advanced on her. "No, please."

I leaned into her face and in a violent whisper said, "I'm not here to hurt you, Catalina. I need to find Cora, and then I'm going to get you all out of here."

She blinked at me, her chin quivering as she asked, "Who are you?"

I didn't get the chance to answer before the sweetest sound that had ever hit my ears came from behind me.

My heart started.

The Earth spun.

And forever began.

One in. One out.

"Penn?"

CHAPTER NINE

Cora

The day Nic died, I remembered not being able to comprehend anything. As I'd sat on the sidewalk, watching them load his body into an ambulance, the cops had spoken to me. Their mouths moved. Sounds found my eardrums. But nothing made it to my brain. Every now and then, I found words coming out of my mouth to answer a question, but it was more like an involuntary reflex than a conscious thought.

My feet moved when I was told.

My head turned when someone was speaking to me.

I was able to prattle off Manuel's phone number to a cop when they asked if there was anyone they should call about Nic.

It was like I had been on autopilot.

The same thing had happened to me when Penn died.

And then it happened all over again the moment I heard his voice in the hallway.

"Cora. Tell me where she is," he demanded.

My whole body jolted, and then my mind checked out.

It was all wrong. Drew was fighting with Thomas. Isabel

and River were hiding in the closet. Catalina had gotten caught by someone in the hallway.

And Penn was outside the door.

My ears started ringing as my hand lifted to the knob.

I couldn't be right. It was impossible.

He was gone.

I cracked the door open. The wide, muscular back straining against a white T-shirt could have been anyone's. But those tattoos? I'd traced them too many times to ever be able to forget them.

"I'm not here to hurt you, Catalina. I need to find Cora, and then I'm going to get you all out of here."

He was…

Alive. Oh, so beautifully alive.

"Penn?"

He spun around so fast that I nearly fell when the tangible weight in his eyes hit me.

"Cora," he breathed, his whole handsome face softening.

My nose started to burn, and he took a step toward me. Instinctively, I backed away. Shaking my head rapidly, I waited for him to disappear. It had to have been some kind of cruel trick Thomas was using to torture me with.

"You're not here," I croaked.

"I'm right here, baby," he soothed in a voice so sweet and so kind that it crumbled reality.

Tears hit my eyes.

I was dreaming. That had to be it.

But I wasn't.

He was too real.

Too perfect.

Too Penn.

I brought a shaking hand to my mouth. "How?"

He curled two fingers in the air. "C'mere, Cor."

I couldn't process any more words. He might have vanished by the time I got to him. Or maybe I was dead too. But no matter what happened after that moment, there was only one place I wanted to be.

I launched myself full body, all at once, into his arms and burst into tears.

"Shhhhh," he breathed, palming the back of my head and tucking my face into the curve of his neck.

I shimmied in his arms. I couldn't get close enough to absorb him the way I so desperately needed to.

The deep baritone of Drew's voice interrupted our rose-colored reunion. "We gotta go. Cops are on the way."

My head popped up, and even though my thighs were still wrapped around his waist, I waited for Penn to cease to exist.

Instead, he replied, "Where's Thomas?"

Drew took his hand away from his head, revealing a gaping wound pouring blood from the side. "I don't know. His fucking buddy caught me with a tire iron. They tore out of here."

I felt Penn's body go stiff.

Penn.

Fucking *Penn*.

Alive, well, breathing.

Penn.

He turned the blue stare that had been haunting my dreams for almost three weeks on me. "Where's River?"

"In the closet," I replied.

He gently set me on my feet, kissed my forehead, and marched over. I knew the exact moment he opened that door, because I was certain her gasp and then the sob that followed could have been heard around the world.

"Penn? Oh, God, Penn!"

I turned in time to see her dive into his arms much the way I had. No DNA test needed.

River wasn't particularly cuddly with anyone but me. With the way she'd been raised, I'd never seen her hug a man. And there she was, wound around him like she too was trying to absorb him.

And, like he had with me, he held her, palming the back of her head and whispering something I couldn't make out in her ear.

Seeing her with him—him with her—broke me in so many ways.

I wanted so badly for that to be real.

For her.

And for me.

I didn't know what the hell was happening or when it would suddenly end, but I never wanted to wake up.

I could live a lie.

To keep that moment, I could live a lie for the rest of my life and die with a smile on my face.

"Mom?" Isabel croaked, shoving to her feet and sprinting into Catalina's arms.

Catalina looked at me and asked the only question I couldn't answer with a truth *or* a lie. "What the hell is going on?"

That would have entailed someone filling me in first.

However, I didn't figure we had a hundred years for someone to explain to me how Penn had overcome the plague of death in order to save me all over again.

"We gotta go, man," Drew said. "And I mean *now*." He reached a hand out. "Cat, let's go."

She looked at me nervously and then moved toward him.

Penn set River onto her feet. The ink on his arm danced as he dug keys out of his pocket and threw them at his brother. "My car's parked three houses up. Change the tag before you bring it back to the apartment."

Drew looked at the keys. "It's a two-seater."

"Just you," Penn clarified. Taking River by the hand, he marched over to me and curled me into his side before herding us both toward the door. "I got everyone else."

Drew stood there for a beat, his jaw tight, flicking his gaze between the keys and Catalina. Then he finally muttered, "Yeah. Sounds good."

Catalina caught my hand as we passed her, falling into step beside me. Her daughter matched our gait as we all power-walked to keep up with Penn's long, purposeful strides.

Somehow, we all made it to the truck.

Somehow, I ended up in the front with my seat belt on— the same with River, Catalina, and Isabel in the back seat.

And, somehow, in the miracle to end all miracles, a dead man got behind the wheel.

I couldn't stop staring at him as he put the truck in reverse.

"How are you here?" I whispered.

He did reply, but not with an answer. "How did he find you?"

Sirens screamed in the distance. "Who?"

"Thomas." He glanced over at me, concern hitting his eyes. "Shit, are you okay?" His big, warm palm came down on my thigh.

I blinked at him some more, waiting for the oasis to fade. "I don't think I am."

"You're gonna be," he promised. "From here on out, you're gonna be."

It was sweet.

And impossible.

"You think he could have traced my phone?" River asked from the back. "They kept 'em locked up during the day sometimes. Do you think he—"

Penn snapped his fingers. "Phones. Everybody's. Now." Three little phones came over the seat. Penn took them all and pulled into a gas station before climbing out. I watched in awe as his long legs carried him to three different trash cans and then back to my door. He yanked it open. "Baby, I need your phone."

I just stared at him.

And then I kissed him because…he was there.

He smiled against my mouth, his hand coming up to cup my face. His callused thumb stroked back and forth across my cheek. "Phone, Cor. I promise we can continue that as soon as we get you back to my place."

"Yeah," I breathed without moving.

And then he smiled, gorgeous and full of life. "Back pocket?"

"Yeah," I repeated.

He kissed my forehead as he dug it out, and then he was gone to another trash can.

And then he was back, the truck was in drive...and Penn was alive.

Shock was weird.

It numbed your mind, only allowing a single emotion to breach the surface at a time.

It'd started with denial when I'd seen him at Catalina's.

But by the time we got to Penn's apartment, he'd yet to vanish into thin air. And I'd yet to wake up. So using the loose formula of A plus B equals C, I'd come to the definitive conclusion that I wasn't delusional.

And it pissed me off more than words could ever explain.

But more, it hurt more than words could ever explain.

He'd left me. He'd lied to me. He'd...he'd *broken* me.

And, now, he was back?

Even knowing all of that, there was still a part of me that wanted to crawl into his lap and hold him for all of eternity.

It just wasn't a big enough part to block out the mounting anger.

"You live here?" I asked when he cut the ignition.

We were in an underground parking garage connected to a high-rise in downtown Chicago. To my left was a white Acura. To my right, a royal-blue Mercedes. Considering I drove a sedan that had run the assembly line when Magnum

PI was the world's sexiest man, I wasn't exactly the most-educated car enthusiast. But even as a novice, I could guarantee that there was at least half a million dollars in four-wheel increments all around that concrete hideaway.

"I bought it recently."

I laughed and there was no mistaking the betrayal laced in my tone as I said, "Good for you. This is a big step up." I slung the door to the truck open, careful not to damage the other cars, and then opened the back door for River. "I guess this means you had more than just a million dollars lying around, huh?"

"I'm sorry," he mumbled.

He was sorry.

He. Was. *Sorry.*

My head was reeling. My heart was simultaneously aching and overflowing with happiness. It was sheer force of will that kept my shaking legs under me.

And he was *sorry.*

I slammed the truck door and walked around to meet him at the bumper. "For what?" It was only two words, but they contained no less than a thousand accusations.

His long, dark lashes fluttered shut for a second. "Let's just get everyone inside and I'll explain." He reached for my hand, but despite the fact that my body was weeping for me to accept comfort from him, deep down, I knew that the weapon never healed the wound.

I snatched my hand away and deadpanned, "I can't wait."

Catalina sidled up beside me as Penn led the way to a small elevator. He did some digging in his pocket for God only knew what and then the doors opened.

We all filed in, like a good little herd of sheep following a ghostly shepherd.

Catalina was behind me, and when the doors shut, she leaned forward and whispered, "Where are we?"

I huffed. "I honestly don't know."

Penn used his superhuman hearing. "I've got a place on the sixth floor. We'll be safe. There's a security firm a few levels down. They keep a close watch on all the entrances and exits to the building. Thomas gets any ideas about showing up here, I won't be the only one pissed."

"And who exactly are you again?" she asked.

"Oh, I'm sorry," I said sarcastically, waving my hand between them. "Allow me to introduce you. Catalina, this is my ex-boyfriend, Penn Walker. You know, the one I've spent the last few weeks grieving, after he"—I turned a wry smile on Penn—"died."

Penn shot me an unimpressed glare. "And I told you I'd explain"—he pointedly tipped his chin up to a security camera—"when we get inside."

I clamped my mouth shut and stared at the door as we rode up. I told myself that the humming in my veins was the remnants of adrenaline.

But I couldn't even lie to myself.

It was the same way my body had always reacted to him—regardless of how much I wanted to hate him.

Biting my lips, I chanced a glance at him out of the corner of my eye. I regretted it immediately.

He was staring at me. His gaze was dark and solemn, but the faintest touch of a grin tilted one side of his mouth. It reminded me of the first time I'd seen him smile. It was that day when we were alone in Brittany's apartment and he was fixing the ceiling fan. It felt like it had been a lifetime ago. But I could still feel the way my whole body had warmed as he'd pointed at his mouth and told me that it was a medical condition.

Nostalgia hit me full force, making my nose sting.

And my temper flare.

"Stop looking at me," I snapped.

"I can't," he whispered. "It's surreal that you're actually here right now."

My brows drew together as I slapped him with a scowl. "I'm not the one who died, Penn."

His grin grew into a full-blown smile, quite possibly impregnating me on the spot. I desperately tried to ignore it—and gave it a seriously half-assed effort to keep my gaze from dropping to his mouth. This task was rendered impossible when his hand landed on my neck. Chills detonated across my skin as his fingers sifted up into the back of my hair.

And then he leaned down, aimed his lips at my ear, and murmured, "God, I missed you."

I bit my cheek as my vision swam. I'd missed him too. So damn much.

But I was allowed to miss him.

He wasn't allowed to miss *me*.

"Don't touch me," I seethed.

Pure Penn. His hand fell away in the next beat—along with his smile.

For a split second, I almost felt guilty. And then, out of the blue, a thought hit me.

"Drew knew you were alive the whole time, didn't he?"

He had the good sense to look sheepish as he muttered, "Yeah."

My stomach dipped, and not in a good way. It was like someone had snatched not just the rug out from under me, but the entire planet. For fuck's sake, was there anyone left who *wasn't* playing me?

"Outstanding," I hissed.

The elevator dinged, announcing its arrival, and I shuffled forward. The instant the door cracked open, I turned sideways, darting out and dragging River behind me.

I assumed Catalina and Isabel were following. But thanks to that hum in my veins, I knew for certain that Penn was hot on my heels.

There was only one door on the sixth floor, so I stomped toward it, my blood pressure rising by the minute.

Penn appeared, waved a little, white keycard in front of the handle, and then pushed the door wide.

My mouth gaped. I had known that the building was going to be nice based on nothing but the parking garage. But, apparently, Penn Walker—the man who had removed my toilet, cleaned mold from inside my walls, and slept beside me on an ancient, lumpy mattress on the floor—had so much money that he couldn't even be bothered with the act of putting a metal key in a hole and twisting it.

Seriously, when was I going to stop being surprised?

"Ohhh, maybe when I figure out what the hell is going on?" I answered out loud.

"What?"

"Nothing," I groaned. "Let's just go inside so I can yell at you."

A slow, gorgeous grin stretched his mouth. "Now, how's a man supposed to resist an offer like that." He shot me a wink.

A wink.

A fucking wink.

Dead men didn't get to wink.

Especially when they weren't really dead.

Penn got busy turning the alarm off while I stood in the foyer. His place was gorgeous. Even Catalina—who'd lived in quite a few mansions before going on the run—whispered, "Wow."

Dark wood floors sprawled the massive expanse of the open living room, dining room, kitchen combination—the furniture being the only thing to delineate the areas. There were overstuffed chocolate sofas. A huge flat screen hanging on the wall. Stone countertops and oil-rubbed bronze fixtures.

But none of that was what made my heart lurch into my throat.

"Hey, you're back," she chirped, her red hair teetering on the top of her head in a top knot as she spun around. With a pint of ice cream in one hand and a spoon halfway to her mouth in the other, her whole beautiful, *healthy* body jerked the moment our eyes met.

And that was the exact moment I lost it.

Again.

"Oh my God!" I cried, racing forward, not stopping until I had Savannah wrapped in an impossibly tight hug. Confusion, elation, frustration, anger merged inside me to create an unnamed super-emotion that made my heart sing, my chest seize, and my legs weak. "Oh my God," I repeated, my hands shaking as I patted down her back like I was searching for an injury. "You're really here." I released her long enough to give her a visual once-over and then yanked her back in. "God, it's good to see your face. How are you doing? Are you feeling okay?"

She laughed, giving me a lingering squeeze. "Yeah. Cor. I'm good."

She was good.

She was good.

She was...

Oh, shit.

After the day I'd had, I was barely on my feet.

However, less than a second later, as the overwhelming weight of reality settled on my shoulders, there was no barely about it.

My knees gave out completely.

CHAPTER TEN

Penn

"Crap," Savannah said as she and Cora, still locked in an embrace, headed toward the floor.

I was already on it. Hooking an arm out, I caught the pair and helped them back upright. Cora was too unsteady to stand on her own, so I anchored an arm around her hips and curled her into my chest.

Like a true asshole, I'd been so entranced in the elevator that I'd forgotten to warn her about Savannah. But seeing Cora standing there with me—no matter how pissed she'd been or how many mountains we'd yet to climb—had been intoxicating.

I'd only thought I'd missed her before that moment.

I'd physically ached to touch her.

To kiss her again.

To hold her.

But not like she was now: a shattered remnant of the woman I loved, dangling in my grasp.

"What is happening?" she cried.

"Shhh, I'll explain everything." Scooping Cora off her feet, I looked to Catalina. "Lock the door. Let me know when

Drew gets here."

She stared at me, concern dancing in her brown eyes, but she didn't argue as I carried Cora down the hall to my bedroom.

In the distance, I heard River squeal, "Oh. My. *God.* Savannah! What are you doing here?"

I mentally groaned when Savannah's response was as to be expected: "Penn's my new daddy."

After kicking the door shut, I carried Cora to the bed, gently set her down, and toed off my shoes before starting in after her. In my head, it seemed like the most natural thing in the world. The two of us had built an entire relationship on nothing but lounging in bed together.

We hadn't gone on dates to nice restaurants.

We hadn't binged on TV.

We'd just lain together, talking, kissing, and spending time with each other.

That was who we were as a couple.

But we weren't a couple anymore—no matter how much it slaughtered me.

Suddenly sitting up, she scrambled to the opposite edge. "No. I need some space."

It burned like acid, but what did I expect? That she'd be so thrilled to see me again that she'd forget the fire, the money—hell, everything about the last few weeks—and welcome me home with her mouth and then maybe her body?

Fuck. After that kiss in the truck, that was exactly what I'd been hoping for.

Dumbass.

Nodding, I shifted directions and moved to the leather

armchair in the corner, perching on the edge like the seat was filled with piranhas. "Are you okay?"

She lifted a finger in the air. "Let's pause on the fact that you're supposed to be dead for a minute and jump right to: Why do you have Savannah?"

"I made a promise."

She laughed in a short burst. "I guess I'm glad that one wasn't a lie."

Shit. She'd been waffling back and forth between being sweet, diving into my arms, and being pissed. But I was really hoping her yo-yo of emotions would swing in my favor.

Again: *Dumbass.*

"Did Thomas—"

"You," she interrupted, grabbing her necklace and dragging it back and forth across the chain. "I don't want to talk about Thomas until I know what the hell is happening with *you*, Penn." Tears dripped off her chin and she used her shoulder to dry them.

The muscles in my jaw tensed. She had every right to be pissed. Hell, she had the right to never speak to me again. But I wasn't about to go down without a fight.

I sucked in a deep breath and put my elbows to my knees. It was now or never. And as I'd learned over the last few weeks, never wasn't an option when it came to my feelings about Cora.

"We can't talk about me without talking about Thomas. He killed my wife."

Her head snapped to the side. "What?"

I cracked my neck. Those twenty-nine minutes had changed my life. I'd obsessed over them for the last few years, and it wasn't until I'd met Cora that I'd been able to spend a single night without being trapped in that bloody hotel room.

I didn't want her to know the man I'd become after I'd lost Lisa.

I'd felt like the old me when I had been with Cora—more than I had in years, if not ever. To me, those moments with her were like a last-minute pardon from death row. She was the first person to give me a reason to want to live again.

But if I was being honest with myself, the shallow and heartless man driven by hate and pain, the liar who had manipulated his way into her bed, was all she'd ever known of me.

And it ruined me that I had to tell her that.

But I owed it to her.

And so much more.

So, while staring into her deep-blue eyes, I finally gave her the truth.

"My name is Shane Pennington. Drew isn't my brother. He's actually my brother-in-law—Lisa's twin—and we didn't get the job at your building by chance."

Her mouth fell open in pure astonishment. "Are you, like, an undercover cop?"

I leaned back in the chair, but only to keep myself from reaching out to her. "Far from it. Drew and I came here to find and kill the man responsible for Lisa's death."

She shook her head. "I…I don't understand. You said the police shot the men who murdered her."

"They did. But those men didn't just break into her room and kill her in a robbery gone wrong the way the police tried to shove down my throat. They killed her for sport. I blew through private investigators, but we never could link the men who killed her to Manuel, Dante, or Marcos. So Drew and I put our heads together and decided to go straight to the source. Drew stole two cars to get locked away with Manuel."

"Manuel? Why would he do that?"

"Because Lisa was nosing around in Guerrero business when she was killed."

She slapped a hand over her mouth. "Oh, God."

Scrubbing my palms back and forth over my denim-covered thighs, I ached to hold her. But if I wanted to get through this, I had to tell her *all* of it.

"We lucked out when he and Manuel became fast friends and then cellmates, but even if Manuel had hated him, being on the inside gave us more intel than we could ever get on the outside."

She shook her head, paused, and then shook it again. She looked like she was in a maze, mentally running into dead ends before backtracking and moving in a different direction. "Wait… So Manuel told you Thomas killed your wife?"

I groaned, dreading this part the most. "No. *You* told me that."

Suddenly coming unstuck from the bed, she jumped to her feet. "I never said that!"

"Relax. Come here." I extended an arm out to her, starving to pull her into my lap, but she sidestepped my attempt.

"Don't touch me. Just *talk*."

I grumbled, shifting in my seat. "We came here looking for Catalina. Manuel had told Drew that his granddaughter had sat in on a meeting where a man had asked him to order a hit on a nosy reporter. We just couldn't figure out who that man was. Manuel only had one granddaughter, and he'd always believed you knew where her mother was. The night right before the fire, when you were telling me about Manuel and Thomas falling apart, all the pieces clicked into place."

She rounded forward like I'd punched her in the stomach. "Oh, God. It was River, wasn't it? She was the one who was there."

I didn't have to answer.

She started pacing. "Oh, God. This is bad. So so so bad. He's going to find out River was the one who told you."

"I won't let anything happen to her. I promise. I'm going to kill him, Cora."

"Oh, great," she smarted. "That makes it all better. That worked out so well when you killed Marcos and Dante." She waved a hand in my direction. "Shit, maybe that did work out after all."

My lips twitched. Fuck, she was cute.

I forced my mouth flat when she stopped and looked at me, her eyes narrowed in bewilderment, not attitude.

"Wait. If you're alive, whose body did Drew identify in the fire?"

"One of Marcos's entourage. I called them. Taunted them about taking over the business. Told them that you and all the women were mine. They sent two men first, thinking I'd be dead before they had to put on their shoes. It didn't work out that way. I lured them up the back stairs. Deleted the thirty seconds of footage of them following me into your apartment and then peeled the stars off your ceiling as I waited for Dante and Marcos to arrive."

"There were only three bodies in the fire. What happened

to the other guy?"

"It doesn't matter."

"It matters!"

I ground my teeth. "You pissed that I took out the trash with those two assholes? Trust me, Cora. We did our research. Those pricks were Marcos's thugs for a reason. They got what was coming to them."

"I don't care that you killed them. If I had a pair of tap shoes right now, I'd do a fucking jig. I am, however, sick of being lied to and kept in the dark whenever you and Drew see fit. So either tell me the goddamn truth, Penn, or you can go back to playing the role of the dead man in this story."

"Fine. I rolled the body out the fucking window before spending the night burying him in Marcos's backyard."

Her mouth opened and closed, but short of a few audible puffs of air, nothing came out. She stared at me for several seconds, her eyes alternated between flaring in surprise and narrowing in disbelief until finally she asked, "Who are you?"

It was the easiest question I'd get all night. "Whoever I need to be to keep you safe." Unable to stop myself, I stood up and, in a few short strides, closed the distance between us.

She immediately backed away, colliding with the wall, and while I wanted to be man enough to give her the option of space, I couldn't. Right then, I was drowning in a different way.

Careful not to touch her, I put my palms on the wall at either side of her head and dipped down until our mouths were mere inches apart. "I love you, Cora. And I don't feel bad about any of it. I was your man. Taking care of you and your girls—that was my only fucking job."

Her breathing shuddered, but her back straightened as she stared me right in the eye and spat, "You were *never* my man."

Blood thundered in my ears as I loomed closer, my chest finding hers, her breasts pillowing between us. My voice was low and jagged as I rumbled, "That's fucking bullshit and you know it."

"I didn't even know your name," she seethed. "My *man* wouldn't have lied to me every minute of every day. Nor would he have faked his own death, leaving me to sink in the pits of grief all over again. Especially not after I'd opened my heart, telling him everything I'd been through with Nic. You lost your fucking mind when I disappeared for a few hours because it reminded you of Lisa. And then you walk out of my life, flipping every last one of my buttons on your way out? No. No way." She gave my chest a hard shove, catching me off guard and sending me back a step. "I'm not an expert in love, Penn, Shane, whatever the fuck your name is, but I can assure you that is *not* it."

"I did that to *protect* you."

"I didn't need protection! I needed you!" She stomped around me. "I was going to school, Penn. I'm *one* semester away from getting my bachelor's in accounting. I had cash. I had plans for a future. I was getting out of there. I didn't need a man to rush in and rescue me. I needed a man to stand at my side and help me figure out a life outside of there. I needed a partner, not another fucking obstacle."

I planted my hands on my hips and breathed, "An obstacle? Are you shitting me? I left you everything you could ever possibly need."

Her face vibrated as she roared, "Everything but you!"

My patience cracked. She wasn't the only one who'd been hurting.

"I couldn't stay." I raked a rough hand through the top of my hair. "Believe me, Cora. I tried to figure out a way to keep you. I don't know where this ends for me. But I know it ends with Thomas dead. I didn't want you involved with that. I couldn't stomach the idea of being another person to drag you down. When Nic died, he left you alone and abandoned."

Her gaze turned murderous. "Don't you dare say his name."

"Tell me your entire life wouldn't have been better if he'd walked away from you a couple of weeks before he died."

"This is *not* about Nic," she snapped.

I stormed toward her, not stopping until our whole bodies were flush. One of my hands splayed across her lower back, the other landing between her shoulder blades. Her chest heaved in time with mine and her eyes were wild, but not with fear.

I leaned in close, brushing my nose with hers before saying, "Oh, but it is, baby. See, Nic was a young, dumb kid who thought he could take his diamond to the junkyard and leave with her still in his pocket. Only he died in that junkyard, and that diamond was stuck there until the day *I* found her. I wasn't doing that to you again. I wasn't dragging you down, covering you in my filth, and then hanging your ass out to dry when something happened to me. I wanted you out of there, despite the fact that I had to stay." I hooked my thumb at my chest. "I watched you sleeping every fucking night for two months with dread pooling in my gut, feeling like my heart was being ripped out of my chest at the mere thought of losing you. But there was no solution. In order for you to escape that life, the Guerreros needed to die and I had to leave."

"But you didn't have to make me think you were dead," she shot back. "Fine, you want the credit? Here you go. You were my knight in shining armor. I should be on my knees, thanking you right now. But you'll have to excuse me. My knees are a little sore. I've spent the last few weeks on them, crying over *you*."

"You think I wanted this? You think I wanted to let go of the woman who made me feel more alive in two months than I had in all thirty-seven years of my life combined? For fuck's sake, the idea of you moving on, making a life with another man corrodes my veins. I know I hurt you, Cora. But I swear to God, I did the only thing I could think of to make your life better rather than making it worse."

She closed her eyes, her entire face scrunching in pain. "Why didn't you just tell me? I could have handled it."

"I didn't want to drag you into this hell."

"I was already in it. Long before you were."

"But I couldn't watch you burn. You might not have been scared of the flames inside me"—I pounded the spot over my heart—"but *I was*. So that connection between me and you had to be severed, no matter how much it destroyed me."

"You?" she accused. Her eyes popped open and the betrayal blazing within them tore me limb from limb. "So you decided to destroy me instead?"

"Destroyed is not dead."

"Stop saying that," she seethed. "It's bullshit. All of it. This was never about me. The day you walked into my apartment and every single day after it, you were one big fucking lie. You swore to me that you weren't looking for Catalina."

"I wasn't there to hurt her."

"No. You saved that for me, right?"

"No," I stated definitively.

Her lips quivered as she peered up at me. "You walked into my life, took one look around, and felt sorry for me? Was that it? You couldn't save Lisa, so you decided to give it another try with me."

Pressure mounted inside me. I wanted to yell at her that she was wrong. Shake her and make her understand. But I really just wanted this to stop. All of it.

"That's not what happened at all."

Her arms hung at her sides, and the emptiness in her eyes knocked the breath out of me. "You made love to me every night, stared right into my face, and lied with your body too."

"Cora, baby. No. I never fucking lied to you like that." I was losing her. She was standing there in my arms and I hadn't even gotten her back yet. But I was losing her all over again. "Please. Just listen to me."

"What else is there to say? The minute you got the answer about what happened to your precious wife, you threw some money at me like a whore and then left."

My whole body tensed, the muscles in my neck painfully straining against my skin. Careful to control my tone, I gritted out, "It wasn't like that. And you fucking know it."

"I don't know anything anymore! Nothing makes sense. Was any of it real, *Shane*?"

I hated the way she said my name. Like it was a curse all

of its own. In a lot of ways, though, I supposed it was.

Because, no matter how much I wanted to deny it, Cora Guerrero had never been in love with Shane Pennington.

Not yet anyway.

I needed her to feel the honesty pounding in my chest, coursing through my veins, and flowing in my lungs.

Taking her hand, I lifted it to my chest, sealing it against me with both of my hands on top. "We are the truth, Cora. We are the *only truth* in this entire fucked-up situation."

Her shoulders rounded forward in defeat. "I don't even know what the truth is anymore."

"Don't say that."

"Then what do you want me to say, Penn?" She flinched. "I mean...Shane."

"Penn. *Please*, just call me Penn."

"Why? So we can continue with the lie?"

My hand spasmed over hers. "It doesn't feel like a lie when you say it. Cora, I'm sorry. For all of it. No, I wasn't supposed to fall in love with you when this started. But you pretty much left me no choice. You're an incredible woman. I knew that from the moment Lisa told me about you. But when I finally met you—"

She snatched her hand away like I'd electrocuted her. "What do you mean when Lisa told you about me?"

I swallowed hard and dug my phone out. "She came to Chicago after getting a tip about some girls getting into drugs and prostitution after answering online modeling ads. The cops weren't doing anything about it, so she decided she would. Through that, she found the Guerreros." I scrolled through my phone until I found a picture of her standing with Drew at a family Christmas party.

She was smiling at the camera, her brother's arm draped around her shoulders. Pictures of her used to break me. Now, I was worried that they were going to break Cora too.

Turning the screen of my phone in her direction, I finished with, "And then she found you."

I saw the exact moment recognition hit her. Her face paled and then her small body turned to stone.

"No," she declared, scrambling away from me. "No, that's not possible. That's Lexy." And then just when I thought I couldn't hurt her any worse, a light of understanding hit her eyes before it shattered her. "Oh, God. Oh, God, you're Shane. You're Lexy's *Shane*."

CHAPTER ELEVEN

Cora

Four years earlier...

"On a scale of one to ten, how bad would it be if we hit a drive-thru for dinner?"

"Bad?" River asked from the back seat. "That would be awesome."

I smiled at her in the rearview mirror. She was getting so old, looking more and more like her dad every day. "Okay, but just this once."

She threw a fist-pump into the air.

I laughed and put my blinker on, cutting across traffic to get into the turn lane. "You find any good books at the library?"

"Meh. Not really. They were all so pagey."

"Ah, yes. Those evil books are notorious for that. Real downer, huh?"

"Total. How'd your test go?"

"Ninety-seven." I brushed invisible dirt off my shoulder. She laughed. "Hey, nice job!"

"Thanks. I got approximately the same minutes in sleep last night, but whatever. I can sleep when we get our mansion in the sky."

"Oh, that reminds me. When we get the new house, I want to paint stars on the ceiling."

My heart skipped a beat. "I can get you some stars to stick up there for now if you want. Or you can take a few of your dad's off my ceiling."

"Nah, those are yours. I want to paint them myself. One in. One out."

Pride soared in my veins. "Yeah. Of course. Any chance you'll let me help?"

"Depends. You gonna let me get a milkshake with dinner?"

My smile stretched as I narrowed my eyes on her in the rearview. "You seriously going to blackmail me like that?"

She giggled. "This is what happens when you deny a child sugar for years at a time. They turn to a life of crime."

Jesus, she was a smartass. Definitely her father's child.

My phone started ringing when I turned into the parking lot of our favorite burger place. "Fine. Chocolate or vanilla?"

"Have we met?" she smarted.

"Once or twice. But I keep hoping to convert you into a chocolate lover."

"I wouldn't hold your breath."

I stuck my tongue out at her as I got into the drive-thru line and lifted the phone to my ear. "Hello?"

It was Brittany, and the panic in her voice hit me like a Mack truck. "Dante's here."

The hairs on my arms stood on end. It was funny how two words could cause such a visceral reaction, but that was all it took with me. Two words and the core of my soul shivered.

"I'm on the way." I dropped the phone in my lap without so much as hanging up first.

"Hey!" River complained when I wheeled out of line. "What about my milkshake?"

"Dante's at the building," I rushed out, my heart going to war with my ribs.

I mentally played out that morning in my head, reviewing my every move. I'd put my textbook away. My money was hidden. That week's deposits were ready to go. River was with me. And all the girls had been accounted for. He hadn't been by in a while, but we were always prepared.

God, I hoped we were prepared.

I glanced back at River and tears were already falling from her eyes as she silently peered out the window.

"It's going to be fine. I'm sure he's just dropping off a new girl," I lied. "But when we get back, I want you to go straight upstairs and lock yourself in your room. You know the drill."

She nodded without looking at me.

"Hey, baby, look at me. It's going to be okay. He has no reason to take you this time." I'd only gotten her back the night before. Manuel had had her for over a week that time. My blood turned to sludge when I thought of him taking her again. "It's going to be fine," I repeated for both of our sakes. "I swear."

"Truth?" Not even her whisper could hide the shake of her voice.

I flicked my gaze to the mirror. I didn't want to lie to her. I didn't even want to tell her it was a lie. I wanted it to be the truth with every fiber of my being. So much so that I didn't hesitate when I replied, "Truth. I won't let him take you."

It took us about five more minutes to get home. As soon as we pulled up, I saw a congregation of women huddled around the stairs and peering up. My heart stopped when ten pairs of terrified eyes flashed my way before I got the car in park. The sound of River's door slamming came at the same time I cut the engine. I scrambled out after her, watching her brown ponytail sway as she ran toward the steps.

"Cora!"

"Cora!"

"Cora!"

I put a hand up to silence them while scanning the group for one I trusted. "Angela," I called. "Go up with her. Lock the door."

She peeled out of the group, taking the steps two at a time to catch up to River.

I turned my attention on Brittany. "Where is he?"

Her already pale face flashed ghostly. "He's with Lexy."

My pulse spiked as fear rocked me back a step. "Shit," I breathed, taking off up the stairs at a dead sprint.

I'd just moved her up to the third floor. She hadn't been there long, but she already wanted out. The girls up there all loved her. More often than not, I'd find them sitting around, waxing poetic about what they wanted to do with their lives. It gave me hope of one day helping them make it a reality. Lexy wanted to get into journalism. She had big dreams of becoming an investigative reporter for one of the major cable networks. Her whole face would light up like a sunrise when she'd talk about it.

But I had to get her out of there first.

When I hit the third floor, I found Angela trying to coax River into our apartment. But she was frozen in the middle of the breezeway, her mouth hanging open, while staring at Lexy's ajar door.

And then I understood why.

"Get off me!" Lexy screamed from inside.

"Shut the fuck up," Dante growled.

There were several loud crashes followed by another scream that echoed around the breezeway, slicing me to the bone with every reverberation.

My mind went to work trying to figure out any possible way in which I could stop this. I could have charged in there, dragging him off her. Dante loved to hit me. Hell, it probably would have been a treat for him.

But with one glance at River, I realized there was absolutely nothing I could do for Lexy.

He would have taken her. He would have beaten me senseless and then he would have taken her again back to Manuel. And God only knew for how long this time.

I was trapped. Caught between allowing a good woman to be raped and abused and losing my daughter to the very same man.

My whole body trembled, and my mind swirled, frantically trying to come up with a solution.

"You fucking whore," Dante seethed.

"No!" Lexy cried.

I lifted a shaking hand to my mouth while tears scraped the back of my eyes like rusty razor blades.

"Cora," Angela pleaded.

I shook my head repeatedly. "Get River inside."

"No," River argued. "We have to help her."

Another scream.

Another grunt.

Another piece of me being stripped away.

My head throbbed with sharp, piercing pain—more than likely my conscience making its presence known. "I can't. He'll take you if I get involved. I can't let them do that again. I can't fix this, baby. I just can't."

Another scream.

Another grunt.

Another knife to my heart.

Like a coward, I came unglued and marched to the door to my apartment. I snagged River's hand, dragging her after me, and barked at Angela, "Go tell everyone to get in their apartments and lock the door. I don't want to see anyone outside until I let you know the coast is clear."

Regretfully, she glanced back at Lexy's door. She wanted to help as much as I did, but no one in that building could afford to go toe-to-toe with a Guerrero.

"This is so fucked up," she whispered before taking off.

Another scream.

Another grunt.

Another blistering wave of guilt.

"Give me your key," I ordered at River when I realized I'd left mine in the car.

She quickly dug it out of her pocket and slapped it onto my palm. Honing my focus on stilling the shake in my hands, I went to work on the locks.

Another scream.

Another grunt.

And then I died. Or at least, I thought I was going to.

"Dante," River called, but she wasn't behind me anymore.

I spun around and found her pushing Lexy's door open.

"River!" I whisper-yelled, lunging toward her, but it was too late.

"Get the fuck out of here, kid!" Dante boomed.

She didn't move, but I watched in horror as she dipped low, picking something up off the floor before shoving it into her back pocket. Then she said, "Manuel's looking for you. He's been trying to call you. Apparently, something's going down on the South Side. He wants you to meet him at home as soon as possible."

"What the fuck?" Dante rumbled, but I heard his heavy footsteps. "Where the hell is my phone?"

In River's pocket.

Shit. I was going to kill that kid.

With labored breaths and a marathon pulse, I clambered across the hall and put my back flush to the brick beside the door. Out of sight but close enough to grab her if I needed to.

"Yeah, don't ask me," she replied in a bored tone. "He didn't give me any details. But he sounded mad."

"Son of a bitch," he grumbled.

I flinched when he tripped over the threshold, almost knocking River over, before stumbling down the stairs. He was high, no doubt. I could only pray he'd wrap himself around a tree before discovering that River had lied to him.

After tiptoeing to the railing, I peeked over and found him folding into his car. I refused air to my lungs until he kicked up a spray of gravel and dust while tearing out onto the road.

I raced back into Lexy's apartment. She was sitting on the floor, her back propped against the wall, her brown eyes wild and distant, blood dripping from the corner of her mouth.

"It's okay. He's gone," my brave, stupid nine-year-old said, squatting beside her.

Her apartment looked like hell. Everything from the couch cushions to the end tables were strewn across the room. Her shirt was torn and her bra was crooked, barely covering her breasts, but I blew out a long sigh of relief when I saw she was still wearing her shorts.

At least there was that.

I kneeled beside her.

She jumped when I touched her arm.

"Relax. It's just me," I assured her. "Are you okay?"

She turned her frazzled gaze on me and whispered, "I got to get out of here. I gotta...I gotta go home before he comes back." Suddenly rising to her feet, she patted her front down, doing what little she could to make her tattered shirt cover her chest. "I gotta get out of here."

I agreed wholeheartedly. If Dante wanted her, there was no doubt that he'd be back. Unless she was gone, all River had done was prolong the inevitable.

Sidling under her arm, I took some of her weight. "Do you have somewhere you can go? Maybe someone you can call?"

"Shane," she whispered before she burst into tears. "Oh my God. I can't tell him about this. He'll kill him."

"Who's Shane? A john?" I asked, guiding her toward the

door, River following close behind us.

"My husband," she croaked.

The air stilled along with my feet.

I cranked my head to the side. "You're married?"

She nodded and then cleared her throat. "I need you to take me back to the hotel."

"Wait. Is this the guy you were running from? Because I don't want you making a hasty decision based on what just happened. We can figure something else out. Get you somewhere safe."

"No. Shane would never... I just..." She stepped away from me. Her hands shook as she smoothed her hair down. "Listen, Cora. I need to leave for a while. But I'll be back, okay? I won't forget about you. I swear."

I liked Lexy.

She was one of the easier girls in the building. She was kind and funny, always willing to help out. Her smile was infectious, and her bright-side attitude was hard not to catch.

Lexy was sweet.

And when I dropped her off at the hotel that night, I looked her straight in the eye and told her the truth. "Please don't ever come back."

CHAPTER TWELVE

Cora

What the hell was happening?

I'd known Penn's wife.

She'd told him about me.

His name was Shane.

Drew wasn't his brother.

Thomas had killed Lexy.

Penn was going to kill him.

He'd already killed Dante and Marcos.

Savannah was back.

So was Catalina.

Thomas had tried to shoot her.

Penn was alive.

And I was currently on my knees in the middle of Penn's ginormous bajillionaire bathroom, dry-heaving into his toilet.

"I'm not a bajillionaire," he said.

Annnnd apparently I was thinking out loud. *Awesome.*

He was sitting, his ass on the cold floor, his legs bent, his feet on the floor, his forearms resting on his knees. Not too close. Not too far away. He was just there in the most Penn

Walker way possible.

"I made your wife a prostitute," I announced.

"She wasn't a prostitute, Cora. She never slept with anyone."

"This is probably the completely wrong time to tell you this, but she brought home a lot of money. Said she had some rich guy on the hook."

He flashed me a tight smile. "Nice to meet you. I'm the rich guy."

"You were there?" I breathed, because at this point, anything was possible.

"No. But she used to video chat with me a couple times a week from that hotel. When she had to head back at the end of the night, she'd pull out cash from the ATM. In a round-about way, I personally paid a few of Marcos and Dante's bills there for a while."

God. My head hurt. It was all too much.

I sighed. "No, you didn't. I skimmed enough money off the Guerreros to cancel it out. Though you probably paid my phone bill a time or two."

He grinned. "I can live with that."

"I dropped her off at the hotel that night," I blurted when I couldn't hold it back anymore.

His heavy, blue eyes lifted to mine. "I know."

"Did she...tell you why?"

"I dislocated both of Dante's shoulders and then slammed them back in socket before I choked him out and left him for the smoke and fire to finish him off."

Holy.

Shit.

This Shane guy was scary.

But I couldn't say that Dante didn't deserve it.

Guilt settled like a boulder in my stomach. "I thought she was going home. Dante came looking for her the next day, but I told him she'd run away. I never considered something had actually happened to her."

"She was coming home. She'd booked a flight for the next morning."

"She never made it," I whispered, emotion bubbling to the surface again.

The first time Penn had told me about his wife, I'd thought it was crazy that he blamed himself for failing her when there was so obviously nothing he could have done. But right then, I got it. Dropping her off there, I'd failed her too.

Reaching over my head, I snagged a decorative floral towel that I knew without a shadow of a doubt Penn had not bought and used it to wipe my mouth.

"I have an extra toothbrush if you want it," he said.

Fresh breath was the least of my concerns.

Settling on my butt, I mirrored his position against the bathtub for two. My body ached like I'd been through a wash cycle, and my mind was a jumbled mess, trying to fit together all the pieces he'd been doling out over the last God only knew how long. Each time I'd thought I had a handle on it, he'd dropped another bomb at my feet.

"Is there anything else?" I asked. "You have some kids or something I need to know about?"

"No," he promised.

"Okay, do you need a kidney and I'm the only match?"

His lips twitched. "No, Cora. All my organs are in good condition."

"Seriously, I can't take any more surprises. If you have anything else up your tattooed sleeves, it needs to come out now. Are you secretly Savannah's biological father come to save her from the clutches of her abusive adoptive parents?"

"What? No. And don't encourage her with that. She's been calling me daddy for weeks."

My stomach rolled.

Apparently, he did have more surprises.

"You've had her for weeks?" I squeaked.

He leaned his head back against the wall. "I got to her as soon as I could. I stalked the hospital for a few days, hoping to see her get discharged. When that didn't work, I went to Cleveland and tracked down her parents. I found her standing on the corner, trying to score some cash. Picked her up and brought her home."

"Home," I whispered sadly. "Right."

He cursed under his breath. "That's not what I meant. Obviously, her home is with you."

At a loss for any other response, I repeated, "Right."

"Truth or lie?"

I picked invisible lint off the towel. "No. That's why I'm sitting here right now, lost and confused, feeling like I was transported into another person's life. I let you lie to me for too long."

"Okay…then truth. My body's about to tear out of my skin over here. Any chance you'll let me come over there and hold you?"

With sadness saturating my vision, I looked up at him.

He was wearing the Penn Walker uniform: boots, tattered jeans, and a T-shirt. His scruff had grown in until it was straddling the line of becoming a beard, and the black tattoos on his arms and hands looked completely out of place in that lush bathroom. But Penn was always beautiful—rugged and unorthodox—and as though he'd cast a spell on me, even knowing what I knew now, I still craved his touch.

"I spent the last few weeks wishing you were sitting in front of me," I confessed, pausing when my voice gave out. "And here you are, but it's like all my dreams and all my nightmares have melded together to form the perfect mind-fuck. I'd love nothing more than to dive into your arms and bury my head in the sands of comfort rather than confusion."

Relief softened his face as he started to stand up.

"But I can't, *Shane*. The man I fell in love with was nothing but a carefully constructed façade, tailored to who he needed to be to seduce me."

"That's not true. It was always me."

"And who is that exactly? Please, I'm dying to know. What parts of you were my Penn with the big heart and gentle touch and what part was Lisa's Shane out for revenge?"

He shook his head. "Me. It's all just me. I didn't show you who I wanted you to see to seduce you, Cora. If you recall, the only seducing I did was begging you to stay away from me for fear that we would find ourselves sitting right here, right now."

"So it's my fault."

"No. Not at all. I just mean I didn't have to pretend with you. Yes, I omitted a lot of stuff about my past and even lied to you about my motives. But every smile. Every laugh. Every kiss. Every touch. That was *me*. That was *us*. And that was the *truth*."

"Maybe. But that's the thing about lies, Penn. They taint the truth until you have no idea what to believe."

A vise in my chest cranked down until I thought my ribs would break. I knew for a fact that crawling into his lap and feeling his strong hands gliding up and down my back would ease it. But what I wanted and what I would allow myself to get sucked into again were two different stories. He'd said that he wanted to protect me. But in the process, he broke me in ways that Dante, Marcos, or even Thomas never could. There wasn't enough of me left to take that chance again.

"I believe you. I think you did have my best interest at heart, but I also think you highly underestimated who I am as a person. All I know for sure right now is that, despite that your heart is beating, Penn Walker died in that fire. And you need to accept that we aren't just falling back into us. I have to figure out for myself how much of the man I loved is left inside this Shane guy, but it's going to take time." I got to my feet and walked over to him, extending a hand down to help him up. "Time that is going to have to wait. After tonight, there is a storm brewing around us. We all need to sit down and figure out what to do about Thomas. There are three girls out there who have been through some pretty traumatic stuff. Our problems don't matter until we make theirs disappear."

He stared up at me, his blue eyes locked on mine. "You don't have to worry about Thomas."

I scoffed. "That might be the biggest lie you've ever told me."

He took my hand and pulled himself up. When he got

to his feet, he gave me a sharp tug, sending me stumbling into his chest. I didn't have a chance to react before his arm snaked around me, dragging me closer until our bodies became flush, head to toe.

My breathing sped as his warmth encompassed me, driving out the chill that settled in my bones since he'd been gone. His chest moved with mine, rising and falling in a synchronized dance as though even our exhales desired each other. He dipped his head, the hairs on his jaw tickling my cheek, eliciting countless memories of his face scrubbing mine as he surged inside me, our bodies fevered and frenzied.

Better judgment told me to back away. I'd asked for time. Thirty seconds wasn't what I'd meant.

But then his breath flittered across my skin, causing a wave of chills to wash over me as he said, "This thing between us was never about truths or lies. We both felt it before the first word had ever been spoken. That day in your bathroom when you grabbed my arm, begging me not to expose Savannah, you might as well have crawled inside me and recoded my DNA, because two seconds later, my life started all over again. You felt it then." He gave me a pointed squeeze. "And I know you feel it now. So take all the time you need, baby. But consider this fair warning: Penn Walker didn't die. I'm very much alive and coming for you."

I gasped when his lips touched just below my ear, igniting sparks inside me.

And then all too soon, he released me and started toward the bedroom door. "I need to make sure Drew got back."

I blinked. Like a million times.

What the hell was happening?

I'd known Penn's wife.

She'd told him about me.

His name was Shane.

Drew wasn't his brother.

Thomas had killed Lexy.

Penn was going to kill him.

He'd already killed Dante and Marcos.

Savannah was back.

So was Catalina.

Thomas had tried to shoot her.

And Penn was alive...*and coming for me.*

What the hell was going on?

"Did you have dinner?" Penn asked, swinging the door open.

I did another round of the blinks.

"Right," he mumbled. "Let me see if I can find a delivery place that's still open. Any preference?"

"Yes. One that can deliver me a new life."

He winked. "I'll see what I can do." He tilted his head toward the door. "You coming?"

I wanted to say no. I wanted to lock that door and crash into his bed, which was probably bajillionaire comfortable and smelled like him. I wanted to sleep for a month and hopefully wake up in a world that made sense. But River was out there, more than likely worried sick. And Savannah was out there, healthy and smiling. And if my memory served me correctly, she was wearing pajamas that actually made her look her age and not twenty-six. That alone was a miracle far bigger than Penn coming back from the dead.

And with all of that in mind, I put one foot in front of

the other and said, "Yeah. I'm coming."

He stood at the door, holding it open until I walked through it, at which point he proved that he had no concept of time whatsoever because he placed his hands on the small of my back.

At which point my body followed suit, proving that it had no desire for time, by arching into it. *Dammit!*

"Oh, thank God, you're back," Penn said as he ushered me into the open living area.

Drew was sitting on a barstool while Catalina hovered over him, putting a bandage over his left eye. I caught sight of Savannah, Isabel, and River huddled together on one of the brown overstuffed leather couches, and when all of their heads turned our way, I shot them a reassuring smile. Isabel and Savannah returned it, but River was too busy watching Penn as though she were waiting for him to disappear. God, how long could I delay telling her that Lexy was actually Penn's wife? She was going to be crushed, and after the last few weeks, guilt was not something else I wanted to add to her plate.

"Is everything…okay?" Drew asked, flicking his gaze between me and Penn.

Penn walked straight to the fridge. "Yeah. Cora needs time. I don't. We'll be fine."

I shot him a glare that I hope singed his chest hair.

His response was to lift a beer in my direction. "Drink?"

I could use a drink. *Dammit squared.*

After stomping over, I snatched the open bottle from his hand. "The jury is still out on whether we'll be fine, *Shane*."

"Penn," he corrected. "And we'll be fine, *Cora*." He

twisted the top off his bottle, clinked it with mine, and then tipped it to his mouth for a long pull. Asshole didn't even try to hide his beautiful, beautiful smile.

Desperate to get away from him for fear that my body's next move was curling into his side, I walked around the island and stopped beside Catalina. "How bad is it?"

She gave me a quick once-over. "It's just a gash. It'll scar, but he won't die."

"Good. Good," I said just before poking him hard on the bandage.

Drew jumped away, cradling his eye. "What the hell, woman?"

I stabbed a finger at him. "That was for lying to me."

He swung a hand out to Penn. "That was his idea!"

"Hey!" Penn objected. "Don't blame me for all of this. You were the one who wanted me to make her think I was stealing all her money."

I bulged my eyes at Drew, switching the beer in my other hand before going in for another poke.

He dodged it. "Shit, stop."

"Oh, this is just the beginning, Drew." I prowled toward him. He backed away, but I kept advancing until I was all but chasing him around the kitchen. "You watched me cry for *days*. You sat there with a front-row seat while I fell apart. You better sleep with one eye open, because when I'm done with you"—I pointed to his bandage, taking great pride in the way he jumped back—"the only scar you're going to have is my fingerprint right there."

Catalina and the girls giggled.

However, Drew's mouth fell open. "Jesus, you're scary."

"You have no idea," Catalina said and then snapped her fingers. "Sit. I'm not done with you yet."

"You gonna be able to protect me from her while you finish?" he asked Catalina, keeping his gaze locked on mine as he meandered over to the stool.

"Probably not," she replied, flashing him a teasing smile. "But if you hurry up, I'll give you an extra layer of gauze for padding while you sleep."

Just as he sat back down, I lurched toward him, my finger poised.

He shot right back to his feet, throwing his hands up to block his face. "Come on. Quit. This isn't funny."

The twitch of my lips on a night when I'd thought it was impossible said otherwise.

CHAPTER THIRTEEN

Cora

"You can fuck right the hell off with that shit," Catalina whisper-yelled while pacing a hole in Penn's hardwoods. Her straight, long, brown hair floated behind her with every turn. "You didn't live with that monster."

Drew's nostrils flared as he watched her every movement, his fists opening and closing at his sides. He'd been staring at her all night. But this was different.

Unable to sit still, he'd abandoned the couch at least twenty minutes earlier and was currently leaning against the wall at the mouth of the hallway, constantly shifting his weight from one foot to the other. "No. I didn't. But I promise you, if the man is still getting an hour of time under my fucking sun and three meals a day, it's too much for me."

I looked at Penn, who was sitting on the couch adjacent to mine. We were on opposite ends, literally as far away as the seating would allow.

"Still nothing?" I asked him, incredulous.

His blue gaze lifted to mine, but he said not the first word. He'd been silent since this argument had started.

After Penn had ordered an army's worth of Chinese food, we'd all gathered around the island, forks in hand, and devoured it—sans plates.

I'd received countless hugs from Savannah and Isabel, while River had mainly kept to herself, that is if you didn't count the way she never tore her suspicious gaze off Penn. At first, I'd thought she was just shocked to see him again, but the longer I watched her watching him, I got the feeling that she was living by the "keep your enemies close" theory. I couldn't blame her. My implicit trust in him had vanished too, but for her sake, I'd smiled as we'd all piled onto the couches with full bellies.

Not long after, the girls had one by one wandered down the hall to Savannah's room and shut the door. They were still awake—hence the whisper-yells. But the "what to do with Thomas Lyons" conversation was in full effect.

Drew wanted to kill him.

Catalina wanted to send him to jail for the rest of his life.

Penn had been quiet, but he'd been clenching his teeth to the point that I'd wanted to Google nearby emergency dentists just in case.

And I… Well, I sat there in my new constant state of being: confusion.

"Under *your* sun?" Catalina snapped, crossing her arms over her chest. "Who died and left you the universe?"

"My *sister*," he snarled.

Catalina's eyes narrowed on him. "Then you know that death is too good for a vile, self-absorbed piece of shit like that. I want him to rot in a cell, with fear terrorizing him the way he made sure it terrorized me. I want him to wake up every morning wondering if it's his last. I want him to pause, his palms sweating and his heart racing, before he walks around a corner. Every time a person passes him, I want his stomach to spasm while waiting for the blow to land in his gut. And God willing, I want there to be a man who teaches him the same way that he taught me that no doesn't *ever* mean no. Too many nights, I lay in bed until the sun rose, my mind tormenting me with every possible scenario of what would happen when he found me. Sometimes I'd even manage to fall asleep only to wake up screaming at the top of my lungs when the fear followed me into slumber. I want all of that for him, because for fourteen fucking years—fourteen *years*, Drew—I've lived like that. It's his turn now."

He cracked his neck and shoved off the wall. "Don't worry. I'll make sure he's good and scared before I slit his throat."

We were all coming at this from a dark and desperate place. Our personal pain and anguish were guiding our path.

Catalina had lived in fear—so she wanted Thomas to do the same.

Drew had lost his sister—so he wanted Thomas to lose his life.

And while Penn hadn't directly stated it yet, I assumed that his reign of terror against his molars each time Catalina would speak meant he disagreed with her. He'd watched his wife be murdered—so he wanted to torture Thomas in the same way.

But I was in an interesting situation. Short of Manuel Guerrero, I hated Thomas Lyons more than anyone left on the Earth. He'd abused my best friend, killed a kind and good woman, and most recently had me arrested and put my daughter into a group home. Whether he ended up in jail or six feet under, it was all fine by me. However, I wasn't driven by unspeakable loss or blinded by hatred. From where I was sitting, all I could see were three innocent people I cared about allowing their emotions to cloud reality.

I'd done that too many times while trying to escape the Guerreros over the years. I'd gotten so pissed or scared that I'd jumped out of the plane without checking to see if I had a parachute. The truth was taking Thomas down wasn't going to be as easy as Catalina storming back in and going to the police anymore. He'd proven that when he'd somehow shown up at Catalina's door, a gun aimed at Drew's face, two of his lowlife pals pulling up the rear.

Nor was it as easy as Drew and Penn putting him in a grave. Thomas hadn't gotten to where he was by being outsmarted. Penn had used the element of surprise with Marcos and Dante, but if what Thomas had said earlier about Drew losing his sister was in fact the threat I thought it was, they were already in his crosshairs too.

Tapping my fingers to my palm, I stood up. "Can we have a timeout for a minute?"

All of their scowls softened when they landed on me.

"I hate to be the bearer of bad news, but after tonight, I think we need to figure out plan C. Thomas knows you're back, Cat. I'd be willing to bet my life that, right now, that man is already working on a preemptive strike against you. It wouldn't surprise me one bit if he already had a laundry list of charges and a smear campaign ready for the moment you reemerge." I turned to look at Drew. "And you. He knows who you are and he's put two and two together with Lisa." I turned to Penn. "Which means he's probably already on to you as well. He's not going to go down without a fight, and while Thomas is the law, he has never once followed it. It's going to get bad. He knows the buttons of every person in this room and I have not one doubt he's going to press all of them in the next few days. So, if we can't even stop fighting amongst ourselves, we're hopeless against him."

Catalina sucked in a deep breath. "You're right."

Drew scoffed. "No, she's not right. She's the antithesis of right. She's so obviously wrong, right won't even claim her anymore. She's beyond—"

"Enough," Penn growled. "Right. Wrong. Purple. Banana. It doesn't fucking matter tonight. It's late. We all need to get some rest. First thing in the morning, we can regroup and figure out the details. But, for now, I need sleep. Catalina, you're in the spare. Drew, you've got the couch. Cora, you're with me."

I laughed, loud and genuine, complete with folding an arm over my stomach and doubling over. "Oh, God, that was funny." I pointed at Penn. "Nice touch there at the end."

He arched an eyebrow, his face stoic as ever. "Who's joking? Let's go. You can be pissed all you want, but—"

All humor dissipated. "Do not finish that statement. Do *not* think for one second that you are going to tell me what I'm going to do. You will lose. Every single time. I'm a big girl, with big-girl feelings and a big-girl brain. I can decide where I want to sleep, and tonight, after the day I've had, that is *not* with you."

His eyes flashed dark, but then, just as quickly, they cut over my shoulder. "All I meant—"

"Oh, I know what you meant. No need to explain. You don't need time—I got it. But I *do*. And that does not involve crawling into *your* bed. So, tonight, Isabel can sleep with her mom, I'll sleep with River and Savannah, and you and Drew can play rock-paper-scissors for the master for all I care."

His lips thinned. "It's only one queen bed, Cora. You'll wake up with bruises you sleep in there with the two of them."

I shrugged. "Better on the outside than allowing you to put any more on my inside."

He frowned—gorgeous and frustrated.

I held his stare—pinchy-faced and perturbed.

Eventually, he gave up, planting a hand on his hip as he turned his glare on the floor. "Christ, you are stubborn."

"Not a revelation." I walked over to Catalina and gave her arm a squeeze. "You gonna be able to sleep tonight?"

She smiled, her whole beautiful face warming. "Probably not, but I'm exhausted."

"Me too."

We started down the hall, leaving the guys alone in the living room. Neither of us had anything to sleep in, but all we really needed were the three girls in the bedroom and a deadbolt on the front door.

Story of my life.

Just before I opened Savannah's bedroom door, I peeked over my shoulder at Penn. He was standing at the mouth of the hall, his smoldering gaze locked on my back. Yeah, I'd escaped sleeping in his bed that night, but I had no idea how much longer that would last. I wanted to be with him—desperately and deeply. But I also needed space to decide if that was even a plausible idea anymore.

He'd lied to me more times than I could count.

But even through the paralyzing betrayal, I could understand why he'd thought that was best.

Unlike most of the men in my life, he'd done it to help me. To help River.

Even to help Savannah.

But whatever his explanation, he'd still done it. He'd still underestimated me. He'd still decided what *he* had thought was best for me, without so much as a conversation. And he'd done it in such a way that left me even more broken than I had been in the first place. I didn't know if I'd ever be able to let that bitterness go.

I finally had a voice.

I finally had opinions.

I finally had choices.

I'd be damned if I'd let anyone take those away from me again.

Drew walked over to him, cradling his fist in the palm of his hand. "I need to go down and smoke. Let's do best two out of three?"

Penn never tore his gaze off mine as he replied, "Get the hell out of my face with that bullshit. I'm not fucking playing rock-paper-scissors with you."

I bit my lip to stifle a smile. However, when Penn's eyes lit and his lips tipped skyward, I assumed I'd failed.

Though, after rushing into Savannah's room without so much as knocking, I succeeded at hiding the schoolgirl sigh.

CHAPTER FOURTEEN

Cora

P enn had been right. The three of us sleeping in one bed had been a war zone. I had a bruise on my ribs from River's elbow and one on my thigh from Savannah's heel. Why I'd thought it would be a good idea for me to sleep in the middle, I'd never know. At the time, I'd wanted to be close to both of them. In hindsight, Penn's bed probably would have been safer—at least physically.

Mentally, I hadn't been able to shut down that night. There was too much to think about. But after spending the day supplied with an elephant's dose of adrenaline, my body was down for the count. I'd done that thing where I'd tossed and turned, convinced I couldn't fall asleep, but somehow, the hours passed in a span of minutes.

Around six, with just over four hours of restlessness under my belt, I gave up in lieu of a trip to the coffee pot. The house was silent as I tiptoed down the hall. Catalina's door was closed, no light showing at the bottom. The same with Penn's, though in a reappearance of my creepy side, I paused at his door and put my ear to it. I didn't know what I was expecting. Maybe a snore or the sound of the shower.

Or maybe the sound of his gruff and hopeless pleas while he was down on his knees, confessing that he'd seen the error of his ways and praying to the Lord for my forgiveness, all the while clutching a photo of me with a Devil-may-care smile, wind-tousled hair, and a low-cut shirt that made me look simultaneously classy and smart but also made my boobs look like I was nineteen again.

I mean, not that I'd given it much thought or anything.

Instead, I heard, "You looking for me?" rumbled from *behind* me.

I jumped at least seven feet in the air—give or take six feet and eleven inches—and clutched my heart. "Jesus, don't sneak up on me like that."

And then that heart of mine, which had just been startled into arrhythmia, stopped.

Because Penn was standing there looking like he'd been ripped straight from my fantasy vault. Shirtless, sweaty, abs rippling, biceps flexing, and holding a steaming mug of coffee like he was the god of caffeine.

I lifted my hand like I was blocking out the sun. "Any chance you could put on some clothes?"

"Not after you moaned like that." He smirked before tipping the mug to his lips.

Annnnnd I'd moaned. *Fan-fucking-tastic.*

Now was not the time to be embarrassed.

Now was the time to crawl back into bed and hope to God that this was a dream and the heat currently licking over me was nothing more than Savannah mouth-breathing in my face. I spun on a toe, ready to make my escape, but he caught my arm.

"Wait, wait, wait. Okay, fine. I'll put on a shirt. I just got back from a run and was about to hit the shower."

Dropping my chin to my chest, I momentarily lamented the fact that his front didn't become flush with my back. Nor did his strong arms wrap around my hips, anchoring me into his curve as he peppered kisses up and down my neck. Only a few weeks earlier, all of that quickly followed by a shower for two would have been in both of our futures.

The regret didn't linger for long when I thought about the pure agony of discovering he was gone and then the earth-quaking elation—no matter how brief—at seeing him for the first time. I knew I'd been falling in love with Penn before that night, but there was nothing quite like losing someone to force your mind to catch up to your heart.

His coffee cup appeared in front of me. "How about I temporarily forgo the shower and you keep that warm for me while I cook you some breakfast?"

I blinked down at the creamy, brown liquid. Penn drank his black. This one had cream—and probably sugar too.

Just the way I liked it.

My nose started stinging. "How long have you been waiting for me to get up?"

He shuffled closer, his warmth looming all around me without him actually touching me at all. "Since the moment you went to bed. I even let Drew take the room last night in case you couldn't fall asleep. I only went for a run to keep from tearing that door off the hinges. And then I've been standing here, drinking sugary milk disguised as coffee ever since."

I choked out a laugh, but it only made my eyes water.

My shoulders sagged, and before I could stop myself, I leaned back against him. He wasted no time wrapping his free arm around me, but not at my hips. His densely tattooed forearm draped over my chest, where he hugged me hard and long.

"Why didn't you trust me?" I whispered, placing my hand on his arm, wishing I could make him feel the hollowness his deceit had left inside me. "I think that's what hurts the most."

"Cora," he breathed before pressing a kiss to my temple.

"I get it. In the beginning, I genuinely do. You weren't there to hurt me. But once you got to know me. After I'd opened up about Nic and everything in between. I just... I can't seem to figure out the rest."

"I'm sorry," he rasped. "I'm so fucking sorry. I knew you were going to get hurt, and I tried to soften that blow as best I could. We both had secrets, Cora. You never even mentioned River being your daughter until you were forced to."

I tensed. I should have known he'd twist this into something he could blame me for. God knew everyone else blamed me for the way they treated me.

But before I had the chance to get mad, he quickly amended his statement. "And I'm not saying that was wrong." Holding the coffee out to the side, he moved around in front of me, his fingertips trailing over my throat and to my shoulder, sending a thrill down my spine.

My breath hitched when he rested his forehead against mine, his hand finding its home in the curve of my hip.

"You believed that people not knowing she was yours was best for her. And you were willing to sacrifice whatever you had to, including hearing her call you mom to make sure that happened. I respect that, Cora. And one-hundred-percent God's honest truth, I do trust you. You're the strongest woman I've ever met. But I am begging you to please take a step back and objectively look at what I did. Lisa was crazy about you. She told me numerous times how selfless and kind you were and how much you helped the girls and encouraged them to strive for more in life. But I had no idea what I was getting into when I met you. You were so much more than all of that. The only thing I ever wanted for you was to make your life easier. It didn't matter if that was fixing the plumbing or hanging ceiling fans or changing the lights in the breezeway. I wanted to give you enough slack to breathe again. I will be the first to admit that I fucked that up. But only because I fell in love with you."

I swallowed hard. He was making sense.

I *hated* when he made sense.

Hated it. Hated it. *Hated* it. Because I knew I wasn't overreacting, but I still felt guilty.

On one hand: Yes, I'd kept secrets. But there was no rule about having to air your dirty laundry on the first date. Yet, he wasn't wrong. In his own way, he'd been trying to spare me. Which, honestly, any other man, any other situation, I would have happily taken the out.

But on the other hand: All he would have had to say was, "You knew my wife as Lexy Palmer," and I would have been on board. She was one of my girls regardless that she was his wife. If she had told him how much I cared about the women who lived in that building and all that I tried to do for each and every one of them, he should have had a little more faith in me as a person.

But hindsight was a bitch. Knowing didn't mean changing.

I couldn't travel through time and shake sense into him before he'd left.

This is where we were at this point.

Him standing shirtless and holding a cup of cooling coffee after he'd spent hours waiting for me to wake up.

Me staring into the blue eyes that had once captured me in their depths—and if I was being honest with myself, I still hadn't escaped. If only I could figure out who I was lost in—Penn or Shane.

"Truth or lie," I whispered. "Which do you want?"

He grimaced like he didn't want either. "Truth."

"I'm really mad at you. And not because you did anything wrong necessarily."

His eyes fluttered shut. "I know."

"I still don't understand a lot of what happened between us. Or how I feel about it. Or how I'm going to feel about it tomorrow. But right now..." I took the coffee from his hand. "Assuming this is still warm, I'm willing to listen to you tell me about who you really are while you cook me breakfast."

His eyes popped open, the sweetest mixture of surprise and relief swirling within. His mouth split into a giant smile that had to have belonged to Shane because I'd never seen one that big in Penn's repertoire of lip twitches.

In one swift movement, he folded his arm around my waist, crushing me against his chest, and then lifted me off my feet. I laughed as coffee sloshed everywhere. And then I laughed harder as I dangled in his arms while he carried me to the kitchen, rumbling, "Woman, I've got a microwave. I can keep that thing warm for the rest of your life."

While scrambling egg whites and frying bacon, Penn started at the beginning—Lisa. Where they'd met. How long they'd dated. It made me a masochist considering she had been the wife of the man I was in love with, but she was also Lexy. Part of me rejoiced in the knowledge that, regardless of how it had ended, her life had been beautiful. He told me all about her sneaking into my room and planting that hidden camera in my stars. I was shocked—and felt a little violated to be honest. I mean, really, who did that? But the way Penn seemed lighter with every detail he divulged made it impossible for me to harp on it. I'd never seen him talk so much or so fast—even through the painful stuff.

Some fun facts I learned:

Penn had gone to MIT—like holy shit, the *real* MIT.

According to his diploma, he was an architect. *Blink. Blink. Blink.*

According to his bank account, he was something of a real estate mogul. The only mogul status I'd ever gotten close to was in the field of bed bug extermination.

He still owned the oceanfront house he'd shared with Lisa in Florida, which was kind of sad and a lot intimidating.

He had paid a guy hundreds of thousands of dollars to buy the identity Penn Walker. Considering he'd paid me a million dollars to escape it, I thought he'd gotten a pretty good deal.

I'd gone into that conversation desperate to learn who he was, but I wasn't ready for the answer.

His favorite color was, in fact, still blue.

But that was where the similarities ended.

However, with a breaking heart and a forced smile, I gave him the benefit of the doubt and kept listening.

After we'd covered all things Lisa, he started telling me about our first few weeks together. It was crazy to hear my memories from someone else's perspective. Some parts were funny. Like when he told me how he'd dropped the first batch of Maury Poppins cupcakes and had to drive all the way back to the bakery to get more.

Other parts were mortifying. If there hadn't been bacon involved, I'd have crawled under the bar when he started listing all the times he'd caught me staring at him. Apparently, I wasn't nearly as smooth as I'd thought.

And then I thought my heart was going to beat out of my chest—and not because I was on my third cup of coffee—when he told me why he never touched my star necklace.

"Every moment with you felt like a reprieve. When I looked at you, when I touched you, when you touched me. Guilt wasn't devouring me. Failure wasn't consuming me. Hate wasn't suffocating me. And on the off chance that you felt the same, I wanted to give that back to you. I'll never be able to forget Lisa, and I don't expect you to forget Nic. But I didn't want to remind you of him. And the minute I touched that necklace, your mind would have jumped to the loss, the pain, and the past. I wanted you with me in the present, where I could protect you from all of that." He'd paused, spatula in hand, one side of his mouth curling adorably, and then finished with, "And only about point zero zero zero *zero* five percent of that had anything to do with me being jealous that he got to you first."

I laughed and threw a piece of bacon at him. (It was a burnt bit. I wasn't a total animal.)

To which I reminded him I was younger than Savannah when I'd met Nic.

To which he scrubbed his face so hard that it looked like he was giving himself a facial.

After we covered all the "how we got here" basics, Penn gave me his backstory.

He was an only child who had come from money and grown up in private schools.

His mother had died of cancer. His father of a stroke a few years later.

He loved to ski—water *and* snow.

He knew enough Spanish to get by.

He'd traveled to six out of the seven continents.

And I was still me.

Cora Guerrero. Single mother, felon, and all-around dreg of society.

I didn't want to feel it. Not with him. But the inadequacy was shrieking inside me with his every word spoken.

Penn had left me for a reason. He'd claimed that it was to keep me out of the line of fire. Protection, safety, blah blah blah. But after hearing all of his stories about the past, learning who Shane Pennington really was, while sitting in his fancy apartment, staring at the gorgeous and successful man,

I had to remind myself that Penn had never intended to stay with me.

And that wasn't a woe-is-me fiesta. It was the truth. He'd said so himself.

Don't get me wrong. I was a real catch. Maybe not when I had two men controlling my life and a building full of working girls depending on me twenty-four-seven—that was a teensy bit of baggage. But I was a good person. I was kind and smart and funny. I had a great ass and quasi-perky boobs, even. But a man like the one in front of me was from a completely different ocean.

He hadn't meant to fall in love with me. His words. Not mine.

And he wouldn't stay in love with me, either. My words. Not his.

In a lot of ways, that realization cut me like the sharpest knife.

But, in others, it set me free, my anger and frustration at his betrayal ebbing into nothingness.

The truth sucked.

But it was a lot like knowing that someone was lying to you. You didn't have the expectation that anything they said would actually come to fruition. And because there was no expectation of truth, there could be no pain caused by the lie.

As much as I hated to admit it:

Shane was the truth.

And my Penn—the most incredible man I'd ever met— was the lie.

I couldn't fault him. I couldn't blame him. I couldn't even be mad at him anymore.

In his infamous words from all those weeks earlier, not all lies were bad.

The one tall, dark, and breathtaking one standing across the kitchen was actually pretty amazing.

And in my world, you held on to any good you could find.

Even if it killed you.

I could pretend.

It wasn't the same, but he was the closest thing to Penn I could ever get.

I could accept this new guy.

Embrace him for however long he decided to stick around.

It was a lie. But I knew it and could prepare for it.

And maybe I'd be ready for it to end when the time came.

I could use him like he'd used me.

Anything was better than the pain of accepting that he was truly gone.

Or so I told myself—for, oh, about sixty seconds.

CHAPTER FIFTEEN

Penn

"What's wrong?" I asked as her face paled.

She smiled—bright, wide, and fake. "Nothing, why?"

"You're looking at me like your boyfriend just walked in and you're trying to play it cool so he hopefully won't notice you, all the while trying to force yourself to focus on me so I won't notice you're watching another guy, either."

She blinked, and the pressure in my chest eased when her face lit in genuine amusement. "Wow, that was strangely specific and yet made no sense."

I laughed. "CliffsNotes: You look uncomfortable and ready to bolt."

She turned on the stool. "I'm not uncomfortable. This has been a good chat. It really helped shed some light on what's been going on between us for the last few months."

It didn't sound good. And I'd noticed that she hadn't denied the "ready to bolt" part.

My suspicions were proven correct when she rose from her stool, stating, "I need to take a shower."

My gut twisted.

Shit. Maybe I'd told her too much about Lisa. Nobody wanted to hear about the ex. But she'd seemed interested and even smiled a few times during those parts. I pillaged through my memories, trying to pinpoint the moment she'd started to fade. Hell, maybe she was tired. God knew neither of us had slept. And then I remembered the half a pot of coffee she'd downed. She'd be lucky if she was tired again this time next week.

I cussed under my breath as she started down the hall. Shoving off the counter, I followed after her. "Cora, please."

She made eyes at me over her shoulder. "You coming?"

My back shot straight, my bones turned to stone, and I froze mid-step.

And, kiddos, that's the story of how I became a sculpture.

"I'm sorry. What?"

She smiled—brighter, wider, and faker. "Nobody's awake yet. I noticed there was a shower in the hall bath. It might be our only shot."

Everything below the belt responded with an *Oh, hell yeah.* Above the belt was a little more cautious. "Our only shot at what?"

She twisted her lips. "Don't play coy with me, Shane."

She might as well have thrown a bucket of ice water at me. "Don't call me that."

"It's your name. I feel stupid calling you Penn." She tipped her head to the side like a cherub, but I knew Cora.

Something was happening in her head. It was ugly and dirty, and I wanted nothing to do with it.

But most of all, I wanted her to have nothing to do with it, either.

161

"My last name is Pennington, Cora. People have called me Penn since high school. And you've called me Penn since the day you met me. No sense in stopping now."

It was a simple, honest statement. When Drew and I had decided to go in search of Lisa's killer, we'd thought the best plan of action was for me not to walk in with the name of her next of kin. Penn was the logical choice.

But something about my correcting her had lit her on fire.

Her eyes flashed wide, and I could see it burrowing to the surface. I didn't know what it was or when it was going to break free, but it was coming and it was going to be huge.

"No sense in stopping now," she mumbled to herself.

"Nope," I replied.

She crossed her arms over her chest. "No sense, huh? None. Not at all."

I mirrored her position, spreading my legs shoulder-width apart, bracing for impact. "Nada."

Her shoulders squared and her neck strained. Swear to God, I think her face vibrated for a second, and then all of a sudden, the ticking time bomb inside her detonated. "It's your fucking name! You are *not* Penn Walker. You are *not* my boyfriend. You are nothing but a fraud." She slapped a hand over her mouth.

This was not how that conversation was supposed to end. The shower, absolutely. But not with her breaking down again. I'd only had her back not even a day, and she'd spent the majority of it crying. Maybe I shouldn't have come back at all.

But fuck that. She was mine.

162

Shane.

Penn.

Whoever I became in the next life. Cora was always mine.

My anger erupted as well. "How am I a fraud?"

"Oh, let me count the ways. Skiing, MIT…" She opened her arms wide and spun in a circle. "This place. My Penn was content sitting on a ratty couch with me. My Penn spent roughly nine percent of his weekly income on cupcakes for me and my girls. My Penn wore tattered jeans and boots."

I made a show of looking down at my workout clothes. "This is hardly a suit."

"How much did those shorts cost, Shane?"

"Stop fucking calling me Shane."

"It's your name! If you want me to accept this new you, then you have to accept it too."

I sucked in what I hoped would be a calming breath. It wasn't. Not in the least. If anything, those few seconds gave me a pause to think. "So let me get this straight. You're pissed that I have a hobby, a college degree, and money?"

"I'm pissed because the last few months have been nothing but a ruse, and I fell in love with a man who doesn't exist."

I planted my hands on my hips and then whispered ominously, "Oh, I exist, Cora." I took a long step toward her, fully expecting her to back away, but she held her ground. And with a few more strides, I made it my ground too. With one hand, I found her hip. The other went to the back of her neck, tipping her head to force her gaze to meet mine.

My frustration ebbed as I took in her pink and tear-stained cheeks, but the moment those life-altering blue eyes of hers landed on mine, she robbed me of all anger.

Sliding my hand around to cup her cheek, I used my thumb to clear the dampness beneath her eyes. "I know I exist because for the four years before I met you and for the weeks since I lost you, I didn't want to. My sole purpose for the last few years has been to make Thomas pay for what he did to Lisa—even before I knew who he was. I breathed because I had to. My heart beat because it had to. I put food in my body because I had to. But it was all just a means to an end. And then I met you. Cora, baby, one minute in that tiny-ass bathroom with you and I more than existed. I was alive again."

I didn't wait. I didn't ask for permission. I just kissed her.

Hard and long. Slow and reverent.

My mouth didn't open.

And neither did hers.

But it was by far the deepest kiss I'd ever offered her.

It was filled with apology.

Hope.

Gratitude.

Regret.

It was words unspoken.

Lies unraveled.

Lost and found.

I kissed Cora with the truth—*all of it*—for the very first time.

She pulled away first, but she didn't go far.

"Penn," she whispered, tears filling her eyes again.

Relief flooded my veins. "I'm right here." I caught her wrist and guided her hand up to rest over my heart. "It's me.

It's still me."

"I want to go home," she cried. "Something has to make sense again. I just want to go home."

I'd pushed her too hard. Too fast. Too much. She'd asked for time, but I'd been so hell-bent on getting her back that I hadn't properly considered the emotional and physical toll all of this would take on her.

Lies were light and fluffy. Made to order. Easy to digest. Impossible to hold on to.

But the truth was dense. A boulder made of magnets, the Earth being the north to its south. The truth could crush a person with nothing more than reality.

And right then, as she face-planted into my chest, it was crushing us both.

Movement caught my eyes, pulling my attention up. Our little altercation had drawn a crowd. Drew, Savannah, River, Isabel, and Catalina were all standing in the hall, concern blazing in their eyes.

I looked at Drew first. "I need the bedroom."

"Yeah. Sure. Go for it," he said, stepping out of the way.

She wanted Penn. She wanted comfort. She wanted something to feel normal again.

I could do that.

"Close your eyes," I whispered.

When she didn't object, I put an arm at the back of her legs and lifted her off her feet.

River's eyes were wide as I carried her broken mother toward my bedroom.

"*It's okay*," I mouthed to her.

She nodded, unconvinced.

Just before I shut the bedroom door, Savannah—God bless that kid—grabbed her arm and chirped, "I smell bacon. Let's go check it out."

When the door clicked, I set Cora onto her feet and kissed her forehead. "Stay there. I'll be right back."

After shoving the nightstand and the armchair into a corner, I snatched all the blankets off the bed and then dragged the mattress onto the floor. On my way to the linen closet in the bathroom, I pulled the curtains tight, blocking out as much of the early morning sun as I could. I didn't have a quilt like the one Cora had used on her bed, but there was a thin blanket that would be close enough.

I spread it out on the mattress and then sank to my knees. "I don't have stars. But I'm here, Cora. *We're* here. Me and you."

She opened her eyes, chin quivering as she attempted a smile. "Penn."

Soft as a feather, that one syllable swept over me.

"C'mere, Cor."

The next beat, she was in my arms, her face buried in my neck.

I juggled her into our talking position: me on my back, her head resting on my shoulder, her thigh draped across my hips, her hand resting on my stomach.

And only then did I exhale.

This whole blast from the past was supposed to be for her. But the soft floral scent of her shampoo filled my senses and carried me back to her apartment too. My body sagged, truly relaxing for the first time in weeks.

"Truth or lie?" I murmured against the top of her head.

"I don't want to play anymore."

"Fine. Then listen to me play. I told you all that stuff in the kitchen because I thought you wanted me to tell you about the man I used to be. I was trying to be as honest as possible, not leaving anything out. But, clearly, I left out the parts you needed to hear most. The parts where I've always been Penn. And I always will be."

Her eyebrows drew together. "That's bullshit. Penn wouldn't ski."

Yes. That's what she said.

She was having a nervous breakdown because I liked to ski.

It made me an asshole, but I laughed. "Yeah, he fucking would, Cora. He'd rent a cabin with his best friend, Drew. Get sloshed on whiskey, lose a bet, go down the bunny slope on a sled in nothing but his underwear, and then wake up the next morning to ride the lift to the highest run, hoping to catch an adrenaline high on the way down."

Her head snapped up like I'd offended her. "Oh my God, Shane wears underwear?"

I laughed again, even when I felt her shooting daggers at me with her eyes. "*Shane* was twenty-four in that story. His mother lived around the corner and still did his laundry twice a week. Trust me, if you had to listen to my mom talk about the scrotal benefits of men wearing underwear each time she didn't find any in the hamper, you'd put them on too."

She peered up at me, no longer mad but rather oddly confused. "There are scrotal benefits to wearing underwear?"

I grinned. "None that I've found. Though if you want to

spend this time scouring the internet to ensure my cock is in tip-top condition, I'll be happy to wait."

Her confusion morphed into a glare. And I fucking loved it.

Because she didn't look sad anymore.

"Okay, so that was your question, and before you argue, I let you get two. So it's my turn. Truth or lie: Why do you want to be an accountant?"

"I told you I wasn't playing." She sat up, crisscrossing her legs in front of her like a barrier. One I ignored as I scooted over until her knees hit my side.

I draped an arm over her legs and gave her thigh a squeeze. "Yeah, but then you asked a question and I answered, so as stated in the Truth or Lie rulebook, that means you are bound to at least one round of ten questions."

She looked at me like I'd sprouted a second head, but that was fine by me.

Because she still didn't look sad.

"There is no Truth or Lie rulebook. *I* made up the rules. And nowhere does it say asking about scrotal benefits locks you into a round of ten questions."

My eyebrows shot up. "Wow, you are really obsessed with my cock."

Her mouth fell open, and it was all I could do not to drag her down and kiss her breathless.

Because not only did she not look sad—her cheeks flashed a sexy pink.

She cut her gaze away. "If you're trying to prove to me that you're still Penn, you might want to stop smiling and making jokes and scowl at me a little more."

"I've turned a new leaf. Nothing to scowl about when I've got you."

This time, not only was she not sad.

Her lips actually started to tip up at the corners.

"Oh, was the other side of this leaf covered in cheesy lines?"

I reached up and tugged on the ends of her blond hair. "Maybe. Is it working?"

And then it happened.

She laughed.

And it was so intoxicating that I laughed too.

The joke wasn't that funny.

It was actually pretty damn stupid. But it was a brief moment of happiness in the middle of a nightmare. I'd embrace it for as long as I could.

She was still laughing when she flopped down beside me onto her back, staring up at the ceiling. "You're ridiculous."

Shifting to my side to face her, I propped my head in my hand with an elbow to the bed. "You're right. I am. And not because I'm Penn *or* Shane. They're the same person, Cora. It's just *me*. We all have different facets to our personalities." I dipped low and brushed her lips. "And every single one of mine is in *love* with you. Cora the grizzly den mother. Cora the soon-to-be accountant. Cora the mother. Cora the chocolate addict. Cora the four-tablespoons-of-beer-and-she's-drunk. Cora the beautiful. Cora the stressed-out. Cora the sad. Cora the happy. I love absolutely all of them."

She blinked at me, her face unreadable.

So much had happened in the last day that I knew she had to be overwhelmed.

But I couldn't take the limbo anymore.

Our journey through hell was far from over. Thomas was still alive. Drew was rip-roaring and ready to go after him. And Catalina was hell-bent about going to the cops. Having some sort of resolution between the two of us would have gone miles in easing the pressure in my chest.

"Say something," I whispered, my heart pounding until I feared she could hear it. "Snatch off the Band-Aid. Whatever it is, just say it."

Her eyes got soft, and while she didn't make a sound, I saw her whole body sigh.

Hope sang in my veins.

And then the tiniest of tiny smiles tipped her lips. "I was right. Your new leaf really was covered in cheesy lines."

I narrowed my eyes, but seeing as to how I'd never smiled so wide in my entire life, I didn't figure it packed any heat. "Were you always this big of a smartass?"

She nodded, inching toward me until her chest became flush with mine, her soft body molding around me. "Yeah. It's one of my better facets."

"What's one of the worst, then?"

She shrugged. "My taste in men."

"Ouch."

She giggled, snuggling in close.

"You never answered my question about why you picked accounting."

"I'm good with numbers. It's an honest living. And it's boring as hell."

"Yeah. I could use some boring right about now."

She hummed but said nothing else.

I stared up at the ceiling in that bedroom, counting her breaths.

One in. One out.

As the minute hand ticked, her body became limp and her breathing evened out.

I'd wanted to talk more. Nothing had been resolved.

But she wasn't sad anymore.

She was cuddled into my side, comfortable enough to finally doze off. Trusting me enough to hold her as she did it.

That in and of itself was further than any conversation was going to get us right then.

And she was cuddled into my side, so this made me comfortable enough to finally doze off too.

CHAPTER SIXTEEN

Cora

The sound of her angry snarl ripped me from sleep. I bolted upright, and Penn lurched to his feet before his eyes had even opened.

"Get your fucking hands off me!" Catalina yelled from the other side of our bedroom door.

I didn't fully process the what, when, or where of what was going on outside. But I knew the who and darted toward her voice.

Penn grabbed my arm, pulling me up short, roughly whispering, "What are you doing? Someone could be out there."

I opened my mouth to say, *Yeah, Catalina.*

But he lifted a finger to his lips and ordered around it, "Shhhh… Stay here."

That would have been fine and dandy if he hadn't magically produced a gun.

What the hell…

"Penn, wait."

He glared at me impatiently and snapped his finger before pointing deeper into the room. "Get. *Back.*"

I wasn't fond of the whole "snapping and telling me what to do" thing, but I was quite attached to my pulse. If he was right about someone being out there, Penn had a gun and I had morning breath.

I was stubborn but not stupid.

Stepping away, I vowed to discuss the snap with him later, like when I was cutting vegetables with a very large knife—assuming I made it that long.

Silently twisting the knob, he cracked the door and peeked out.

I held my breath, my hand at my star as I started doing the math on where River could be in the apartment. I'd vaguely remembered seeing her and Savannah in the hall just before my countless emotional breakdown of the day.

Then my back shot ramrod straight as Drew's growl floated into the room.

"You need to chill the hell out."

Penn's shoulders sagged and he blew out a ragged exhale, yanking the door open. "Jesus fucking Christ. What the hell are you two bickering about?"

Relief surged through me—prematurely.

"Oh, good. You're awake," Cat snapped, pushing past Penn. Her brown eyes landed on me, the light from the hall revealing an alarming amount of anxiety. "Get your shoes. We're leaving."

"The hell you are," Penn rumbled.

"You guys can have Thomas," she told Penn. "Kill him. Skin him alive. Hang him from the courthouse steps, I don't give a damn." She pointed at me. "But she and I, and all the kids, are leaving. *Now.*"

My stomach twisted. Catalina wasn't known to be dramatic. She hurt, she cried, but she wasn't Debbie Doomsday. So whatever had set her off had to be bigger than big, and it made me nauseated before I even knew what it was.

"What's going on?" I asked. Penn moved to my side, his arm going around my stiff shoulders, but I only had eyes for Catalina. "Tell me."

She looked at Penn's possessive hold on me and flashed Drew a pointed glance before starting in. "Early this morning, a judge granted my father a temporary release to attend his sons' funeral. As of twenty minutes ago, the correctional officer who was guarding him was found dead, with no sign of Manuel anywhere. It's all over the news. A full manhunt is underway."

My head spun as the blood drained from my face. Penn was there to keep me on my feet, but who was going to keep the world from falling out of orbit beneath us all?

"This doesn't mean anything," Drew said, propping his shoulder against the doorjamb, but he was anything but relaxed. His gaze was fixed on his friend, a silent conversation happening between them.

Catalina spun around. "Are you kidding me? In the wee hours of the morning, after my husband finds me for the first time in four years and fails to kill me, a judge signs off to have my father temporarily released from prison? Please tell me you are not stupid enough to think this is a coincidence."

He rolled his eyes. "Thomas put Manuel away. Why the hell would he let him out now?"

"Shit, you *are* that stupid." She slanted her head. "How have you made it this far without a brain?"

He arched an eyebrow. "Good looks and big cock. You?"

Penn and I watched their conversation like a tennis match. They'd known each other less than a day and it was already safe to say there was no love lost between the two of them.

"Jesus Christ," Penn muttered. "Would you two can it for a minute? Catalina, talk."

She flipped Drew off before turning to Penn. "Riddle me this. If my body was found fresh and floating in a river, who would the police assume killed me? The shattered district attorney with a golden reputation or my felon father who I testified against and has since killed a guard and escaped custody?" Panic settled in my stomach as she pointedly looked to each one of us. "Any guesses?"

"He's the fall guy," I replied, taking my own weight again. "Holy shit. Not only did he just paint an even bigger target on your back, he somehow took the heat off his own."

"Bingo!" Catalina chirped, tapping the end of her nose.

My heart picked up a marathon pace as all the pieces started snapping together. "Oh. My. God." I leveled my panic on Catalina. "Do you think—"

"Yep. Dear old daddy is sixty-five now, but even at sixty-one, he was in shitty health. Arthritis, too many years of drugs he passed on to Dante, too many extra pounds putting pressure on his knees. His mind is sharp, but physically, he's ninety with one foot in the grave. No way he overpowered a guard and killed him alone."

The room went static.

Penn stood taller.

Drew shoved off the jamb.

The hairs on the back of my neck prickled.

And Catalina stared at me, waiting for me to come to the same conclusion she'd already concluded.

"They're working together again," I breathed. "Thomas and Manuel. The staged escape and murder keep Thomas's hands clean, but it gets a Guerrero back in play." Not even Penn's warmth could block out the chill in my veins. "Oh, God, he knows who you are." I lurched away from him. "Oh, God, he knows who you both are. We gotta get out of here. We gotta leave—*now*." I bolted toward the door, calling, "Get the girls ready!" I made it exactly two steps before a tattooed forearm around my hips yanked me back.

"What the fuck are you doing?" he snarled.

With frenzied hands, I pushed at his arm. "I have to get them out of here!" I looked at Catalina. "We need to go get the money out of the storage unit and run."

"Agreed," she replied with a curt nod.

It was followed by a boomed, "No fucking way!" Penn swung around in front of me. "You're not going *anywhere*."

"Move," I snapped, doing my best to sidestep him with no luck.

"You've lost your goddamn mind if you think I'm going to stand here and watch you leave. I just fucking got you back."

Frustration overtook me. "And who said you got me back, Shane?"

His face got hard as his whole body swelled with anger. "You did. The minute you fell asleep on my chest, your hand clinging to my shirt like you were afraid I was going to disappear, your body inching closer until you were on top of me, and breathing my name—and not fucking Shane, but my real name."

"It's not your real name!"

"It is because *you* called me that. I was no one before I walked into your apartment. You made me Penn. And because of that, I'm fucking yours. So don't you dare tell me you didn't come back to me. You can be as pissed as you want, as hurt as you want, as bitter as you want, but you felt it, Cora. The same way I did. The same fucking way we have *always* felt it."

He was right. I'd always felt it with him even before I had known what that *it* was. But feelings didn't change our circumstances. The truth didn't make the lies disappear. And as much as I would have given anything to believe otherwise, love didn't always conquer all.

"You have made every single decision for me for the last few months, and while some of those turned out great, others did *not*. I'm sick of letting everyone else dictate my life. Thomas is doing it. Manuel now too. And I'll be damned if I'm going to let you join that cast."

"I'm not trying to run your life. I'm trying to keep you from running *out* of mine." He raked a hand through the top of his hair. "We can figure this out. Manuel is not the be-all and end-all. There's no need to run anywhere. Not when we're together."

"Whether it's now or later, it's going to happen one way or another."

"No. It's not. I won't let it. I am sorry, okay? I've told you that in every way I know how, but let me try it again. I fucked up, Cora. I admit that. But I can't let you leave now. And that's not me trying to run your life or make decisions for you. That's me trying to be your partner."

I'd thought about why I was mad at Penn a lot over the last day.

First, it was because of all the lies. Because... well, duh. That was never cool.

Then I thought it was because of more lies, specifically the ones where he wasn't Penn but actually this rich, vigilante guy named Shane.

But right then, the real reason my heart was broken into a million pieces flew from my lips with the velocity of a nuclear warhead. "Until you leave again!"

His head jerked back. "What?"

"Okayyyyy," Drew drawled. "I think Cat and I are going to give you two some privacy." He ushered her out, leaning back in to say, "Penn, man, think about the house in Florida." He tapped the doorframe twice, shot me a wink, and then shut the door.

Through it all, Penn never tore his irate gaze off me. "What do you mean until I leave again? I'm not going anywhere."

I let out a resigned sigh. "Come on. Let's be real here. Once all of this is said and done, you're not going to be here."

"Oh, really?" he asked. "And where the hell am I going to be?"

I swung my arms out to my sides, slapping my hands against my thighs as they fell. "I don't know. Skiing?"

His eyebrows pinched together. "What is it with you and skiing?"

"I don't like skiing. That's what it is."

178

"You ever been?"

"No."

"Then how do you know?"

"Because it's expensive."

"So it's a money thing?"

"No, it's a people thing!"

He scratched the back of his head. "Yeah, okay, I have no idea what we're talking about right now."

I groaned at his inability to follow the oh-so-obvious bouncing ball. "Have you ever seen *Pretty Woman*?"

His eyebrows popped so high that they nearly hit his hairline. "Unless this is your way of telling me that you've been working the street with the girls over the last few months, that's not helping clarify anything for me."

"I'm not like you, okay? We don't have the same interests. We don't even come from the same world. When this is all over, you're going to realize how different we are."

I was on the verge of more tears.

But Penn... Well, he smirked, dark and sexy. "Jesus, Cora. Now *this* I can handle."

"Oh, fantastic. Handle away."

He smiled. "Any chance you'll come lie down with me so I can properly explain all the ways different can be good without you trying to put space between us like a chastity belt?"

Per my body: *Yes. Absolutely yes.*

Per my mind and thus my mouth: "I'm not sure that's a good idea."

His eyes twinkled with mischief. Taking my hand, he took a few steps back, pulling me with him. "Okay, well, that's definitely a difference that we have. Because I think it might be the best idea I've had in a while."

"No offense, Penn. But your last idea was faking your own death. I don't think there's a lot of competition in the great-ideas-you've-had-recently category."

His smirk grew into a smile, and he continued backing up. "So you admit it's a great idea."

"Actually, I'm pretty sure I said the opposite of that."

My pulse quickened when his heels hit the mattress.

His teasing gaze became heated, which sent a rush through my nervous system. God, I'd missed that feeling. It was like stepping out of the shade and into the sun. I'd thought I'd lost it when I lost him.

But he wasn't gone.

He was standing right there in front of me.

His hand went to the back of his shirt and then he was suddenly standing right in front of me *shirtless*. "I personally think we need to strip this differences business down to a *very basic level.*"

CHAPTER SEVENTEEN

Cora

My breath caught in my throat when his callused hand went to the hem of my shirt.

"You can tell me to stop, Cora. And you know I will. But I'm begging you not to."

He was so close that I was hopeless to prevent my body from responding. The hum hit me with a deafening force, tingling my skin as though the air between us had become electrified.

I peered up into hooded, blue eyes. "I don't think this is going to fix anything, Penn. We have too much stuff to worry about."

Okay, not totally true. Jumping him right then and there would have done wonders to fix the ache between my legs, but it wouldn't have changed who we were.

Or who we weren't.

"That's because there's nothing to fix. And stop worrying. I'm right here." He slid my tank top up a few inches, revealing my stomach. "So I'm going to repeat: You can tell me to stop, Cora. And you know I will. But I'm begging you not to."

"I don't want you to stop, Penn. I've never wanted you to

stop. Even when you did."

His eyes got soft.

And then I lost sight of them altogether.

His lips came down, sealing over mine, crumbling the resistance I'd never had.

He kissed me breathless, even more so than the first time I'd tasted him. His mouth opened, our tongues gliding together, stealing my thoughts—and fears.

Pressing up onto my toes, I circled my arms around his neck, deepening the kiss until I decided I couldn't get close enough and started climbing up his body.

He palmed my ass, lifting me off my feet. My legs curled around his hips, a moan escaping as I found glorious friction against his stomach.

I waited for him to fall back, take me to our mattress on the floor, and erase the last few weeks of blistering pain with nothing but his body.

Instead, he murmured a curse and started walking with me held tight in his arms.

"Where are you going?" I murmured, moving my affections to his neck.

"I heard Drew snoring through that door last night. I'm not going to be quiet, Cora. And I sure as fuck don't want you to be, either."

I smiled when I realized we were in the bathroom. He kicked the door shut and set me onto my feet. He went straight to the giant jetted tub and flipped the faucet on. My stomach dipped at the idea of riding him with the water sloshing waves around us. However, like a tornado, he spun around the room, hitting the shower—both heads—and the sinks on the double vanity until I wasn't certain if we were going to have sex or flood the building.

"What are you doing?" I laughed.

He put his hand to his ear and then tossed me a wink. "That should be good enough." Curling a finger at me, he said, "Come here, baby. I want to show you something."

My cheeks heated as I sauntered toward him.

He pecked me on the lips and once again caught the hem of my shirt. "May I?"

I lifted my arms above my head. "Such a gentleman."

"For now." He smiled, tugging the fabric over my head and tossing it absently across the room. Raking his teeth over his bottom lip, he stared down at his finger as he traced the swells of my breasts.

Goose bumps pebbled my skin as a chill ricocheted through me. I hissed, my lids fluttering shut, when his callused finger dipped inside the cup of my bra and brushed against my hard nipple, sending sparks straight to my clit.

"Oh, God," I breathed.

He moved to my other breast, repeating the mind-numbing process as he proved he was a multitasker by unhooking my bra at the same time.

"Show-off," I murmured, allowing it to fall down my arms to the floor.

I felt his smirk as he trailed kisses up my neck to my ear, where he rasped, "Give me your hand." I offered it palm out, and he placed it on his chest before ordering, "Now, give me your other hand."

I followed his direction and this one landed on my naked breast.

He covered my hands with his own, using our connection to kneed and rub. "How does that feel, baby?"

I arched my back and tried to slide out from under his grip. "Better when you do it."

"No. *How* does it feel? Two chests, but they're *different*, right?"

My eyes popped open and I swallowed hard. "Penn...I—"

"Shhhh." He lifted the hands we'd had over his heart to his mouth and kissed each of my fingertips, rubbing the last back and forth over his bottom lip. "What's this, baby?"

"Your mouth."

He smiled, moved my hand off my breast, and plucked my nipple—rough and intoxicating. "And this?"

"My nipple," I replied breathlessly.

"So we have my mouth and your nipple. Two *very different* things. Let's see how this works out between the two of them."

My lungs burned with anticipation as he slowly sank down, his blue eyes aimed up at me, and sucked my nipple between his lips.

"Oh, God." I used his shoulders for balance as I swayed on boneless legs.

Lost in sensation, I closed my eyes, but he pulled his attention away all too quickly.

"No, Cora. I want you to look at me. I want you to see exactly how beautiful *different* can be."

I cried out in the most incredible mixture of pain and pleasure as his teeth raked across my sensitive flesh, which he followed with bold caresses of his tongue swirling and soothing.

His eyes were locked on mine, beautiful, hypnotic, and powerful, and he greedily switched his focus to my other breast. That first nip ignited a fever across my skin, heating me from head to toe.

Nipples to clit.

"Penn," I begged, his intentions being clear when he thankfully started on the button of my jeans. I worked with him, shimmying them down my thighs as best I could without breaking the connection of his mouth at my breast.

I'd just stepped out of cumbersome denim when he swept my panties aside and trailed his agile finger over my slit, dipping into the wet without pressing inside.

"Yes," I hissed, spreading my legs, silently asking for more.

It was an offer he accepted with enthusiasm, slipping two fingers inside me.

"Oh, God, baby, yeah, please, yes," tumbled from my lips in a string of incoherent ramblings.

"My fingers and your heat, Cora," he murmured against my breast. "You feel that?"

"Yes."

He curled his fingers, stroking and coaxing my release to the surface. "Does different feel good, baby?"

"Yes," I replied wantonly, only capable of single syllables.

"Different feels good, huh?"

I moved my hand to the back of his head, urging him to take more of my breast. His mouth opened wider, and he sucked me deep. His approving groan vibrated my nipple, sending a sinful charge roaring through my already blazing body.

"Very," I answered.

I silently lamented answering him when he suddenly rose to his feet and stepped away.

His smoldering gaze raked over me, an arrogant smirk pulling at his lips. "She fucking looks like this and is freaking out like I'm the prize."

My cheeks heated under his praise.

"And she's cute." He hooked his thumbs into the waistband of his shorts and shoved them down, his long and thick erection popping free. "Mmmm," he hummed, drawing my attention back to his smiling face. "And she looks at me like that. Jesus, woman. You're going to kill me."

"Well, technically—"

"You make any kind of joke right now about me already being dead and I'm putting my shorts back on."

I flashed him my own arrogant smirk and shrugged. "Well, Penn is already dead, sooo..."

He shook his head and mumbled, "And she calls my bluff."

I laughed as, all at once, he scooped me off my feet and carried me into the shower. It was so big that there wasn't a door or a curtain. There was a head on each end, raining water down from the ceiling. But I was eyeballing the long bench that ran the length of the wall.

He set me onto my feet under the spray and grabbed a bottle of body wash off the stone shelf in the corner. "I need a shower. And to fuck you something fierce, but first, we need to finish out the discussion about us being different."

My stomach dipped, and my nipples peaked. "I think I like your differences game more than Truth or Lie."

"Me fucking too," he replied, doing a quick scrub-a-dub-dub routine before turning his soapy hands on me.

I smiled, giving him my back, but his hands went right back to my breasts.

"I've missed showering with you. I'm always so much cleaner when you do it," I said.

His chest hit my back and the whiskers on his chin tickled as he peppered kisses up my neck. "I don't know about how clean I'll get the rest of you, but these"—he rolled my nipple between his thumb and his forefinger—"will be spotless."

"Mmm," I moaned, leaning my head back and closing my eyes. The water poured down over us, rinsing the soap away as the pressure between my thighs swelled like a wave ready to crash.

"Give me your hand, Cor."

I obeyed immediately, eager for where this one was going to land. He shifted to my opposite side and guided my fingers between my legs. The air tore from my lungs as I found my clit, the gripping sensation building in my stomach.

"What do you feel?" he whispered, nipping at my ear.

"Me," I replied, lulling my head to the side to rest on his shoulder.

His fingers joined mine, teasing and playing before entering me slowly, stretching with deliberate intent.

My hand stilled as I folded forward, gasping for air—and release.

"Don't stop," he demanded.

I was panting, close but so far away from any kind of release, when he guided my free hand to his length, wrapping my palm around his shaft and folding his on top.

The sexiest hiss sailed from his lips as I slid him through my fist. The muscles in his chest strained against my arm as we worked his length together.

"What do you feel?" he asked in a husky voice.

"You," I replied, tilting my head back, asking for a kiss.

His lips came to mine, but not for a kiss. He thrust his finger deep inside me, inciting an explosion of pleasure that shook the Earth. Releasing his length, he snaked his arm around me to keep me on my feet and whispered into my open mouth, "Different can be beautiful. We came from different worlds—I will give you that. But I lived in yours, and now, you're going to live in mine. Because we *belong* together."

"Penn!" I cried, my orgasm rearing up.

His finger pumped inside me, twisting and turning as he drove me to the edge. He nipped at my bottom lip. "We earned this. You and me. We earned this feeling, right here, right now. And we earned it in the hardest fucking way possible. It wasn't easy and I don't suspect it ever will be, but dammit, we're gonna be together."

I swallowed every one of his words.

They tasted like hope—my greatest enemy of all.

"Please, Penn," I begged, the curling ache of need pulsing to the point of insanity. I needed him. I needed him in so many ways. The void only he could fill within me wasn't just sexual.

It was in my heart.

It was in my soul.

It was in my being as a whole.

It was just him.

That's all it had ever been since the day we'd met.

Shane. Penn. I didn't care. It was just *him*.

He continued, emotion overtaking him, filling not only his words but his movements with a desperate urgency. "We were the only truth that mattered in any of this. We earned this. I won't lose that. I won't lose *you*."

"No!" I cried when he suddenly withdrew his fingers as I was teetering on the edge of orgasm. But I had no time to complain because, in one fluid movement, he spun, sank onto the bench, pulled me down into his lap, his front to my back, and impaled me in the most erotic experience of my life.

"Penn," I choked out as the orgasm tore from my body like it had been ripped from my soul.

He roughly closed my legs, holding them shut with his thighs. Then, circling his arms around my waist, he used his upper-body strength to fuck me from the bottom with the hard and fast rhythm of determination. My clit rolled between my clenched thighs, sending me higher and higher through the volatile peaks and valleys of ecstasy.

"I love you," he growled, his fingertips biting into my hips as he drove into me. "I love you so goddamn much. I will not give up on us again. Promise me you won't, either. *Promise me*, Cora."

I was coming down from one orgasm and could feel him swelling impossibly harder as he started his own climb to the top. The last thing I wanted was for his desperation to linger when he got there.

I felt beautiful with him.

I felt safe with him.

I felt loved with him.

I always had.

And the blood hummed in my veins in a way that I knew it would never disappear.

Not with him.

"Stop," I breathed and it was like I'd flipped a switch.

His legs opened, his arms fell away, and he leaned back so not even his chest was touching me.

God. This man.

This sweet, sweet broken and beautiful man.

The one who loved me and had only been trying to take care of me—albeit a little misguided sometimes. And yeah, so what—he was loaded and liked skiing. I liked money, and while I'd probably break my face on a slope, I'd be more than happy to drink hot chocolate and watch him.

There was no denying that we came from different worlds. But he'd never judged me or made me feel bad or dirty about where I'd come from. And I had a sneaking suspicion that it didn't matter whose world we settled in as long as we were together.

"I'm sorry," he said as I climbed out of his lap, the steam from the shower causing my skin to pebble.

I turned around, finding his strong and handsome face filled with apology.

"Are you—"

"I'm fine." I smiled, putting a knee on either side of him and then climbing back into his lap.

He brushed my wet hair off my neck and then traced it up to cup my cheek. "Jesus Christ, you scared me."

I leaned down to peck his lips, where I murmured, "Come back inside me, baby. I just wanted to have this conversation face-to-face."

His eyes darkened, and he didn't delay in guiding his length into my opening. Holding his gaze, I sank down, slow and steady.

He bit out a curse as I took him completely—base to tip.

"Fuck, Cor," he murmured, leaning forward for a kiss I denied him.

"Promise you'll never lie to me again."

He stared back at me, hope filling his eyes. "I swear."

That one was easy. I feared that the next one might be where we ran into issues. "And promise me you won't kill Thomas."

His whole body jerked. "Cora, I—"

"I can't chance losing you again. I just can't." Tears welled in my eyes. "You promised you wouldn't lie to me. So if this is what you're planning—"

"Hey, hey, hey. Shhh... Relax. I'm not going after Thomas again. It's not worth it. *He's* not worth it. But *we* are, okay? We'll figure it out. As long as he can't touch you, I'll learn to accept whatever happens to him."

It was my turn to jerk. "That easy?"

He scoffed. "*No.* There was nothing easy about this decision. But living without you for the last few weeks, then getting you back... Well, it's put some serious shit in perspective for me."

"Was I the serious shit or the perspective?"

His lips twitched. "Both, smartass."

I smiled and it forced a tear from each of my eyes.

He groaned and brought his hand up to clear my face. "Any chance you can stop crying and talking about Thomas while my cock is inside you? There is a solid chance I'm about to go limp."

Laughing, I leaned forward and kissed him, deep and reverent.

"And one more thing," I murmured.

He rolled his hips, proving that there was nothing limp about him. "Make it fast, baby."

"When this is all over and you buy us a completely ostentatious house, I want a shower like this one. And—okay, so two more things—you have to promise that River can paint stars on the ceiling in her room."

Penn was rugged and handsome—the picture of pure masculinity. But, right then, a huge boyish grin lit his face. "You moving in with me?"

I shrugged. "You kinda burned my apartment down."

"I did," he said proudly. "I so fucking did."

I lost his length as he stood up, but I gained so much more as Shane Pennington—my Penn—laid me down on the tile floor of his shower, the warm water flowing over us and washing the lies down the drain, and made love to me for the very first time.

CHAPTER EIGHTEEN

Penn

"Relax. I'm not driving you off a cliff. I'm not sure if anyone's told you this, but there is humankind outside of Chicago," I told Cora as we pulled out of the parking garage.

Unconvinced, she nodded, anchored her hand to my thigh, and went to work worrying her necklace like she had a vendetta against it.

Twenty hours later, while the gate slid open, revealing the tall, three-story house I'd shared with Lisa, *she* was offering *me* reassurance.

"Relax. I'm right here."

We left Chicago the very same day as the news broke about Manuel.

He was still on the loose. But, regardless of how small the world felt sometimes, it was actually a very large place. So, rather than sitting around and waiting for Thomas to make his move, we'd decided to take the girls and get the hell out of Dodge. If Thomas wanted to find us, he would. Same with Manuel. But I sure as hell was going to make him bring it to my turf—a state where he had little to no connections.

Nothing like thirteen hundred miles to level the playing field.

Going down to Florida had actually been Drew's idea. Initially, I'd balked at the thought of going back there. I wasn't real eager to bring Cora to the house I'd shared with Lisa. But it was big enough for all of us, furnished, and far enough away to give us time to figure out our next move.

He hadn't said it yet, but I knew Drew well enough to see that he had no intention of staying in Florida. While Cora and the promise of a future together had rearranged my personal priorities, Drew still had his heart set on vengeance. I had not a single doubt that, one day, we were all going to wake up to find him gone. This meant, if I was going to try to talk him out of going after Thomas alone, I had to act fast.

We weren't sure what to do with Catalina's information yet. If Manuel was out there, gathering the troops, our taking Thomas down in the eyes of the law was only going to put a bigger spotlight on Catalina. The media would have had a field day with that story.

Our best bet was to lie low for a few days, maybe a week, and see if the cops could do their damn jobs for once. If we could get Manuel out of the picture again, I was willing to do whatever I had to—including knocking his ass out—to keep Drew from going after Thomas before Catalina had the shot.

Drew wasn't my brother according to DNA, but he was my family all the same. I couldn't stand the idea of losing him. That was part of the reason why all those years ago, when we'd first decided to find Lisa's murderer, I'd declared that I was the man who was going to kill him.

Yes, I absolutely, with my whole heart, wanted that

asshole dead.

But I didn't want Drew going down for it.

I shot Cora an appreciative smile, lifted our joined hands to my lips, and kissed her knuckle.

She was actually there.

A few days earlier, having her at my side again was more than I'd ever hoped for.

Though I'd never once considered bringing her to this house. Much less bringing *all* of them.

"Holy crap," River breathed from the back seat.

Which was followed by Savannah saying, "Daddy, I'm going to need a bathing suit. Stat."

Isabel giggled, but much like during the entire trip down, she didn't say anything. The kid was quiet. Eerily so. But then again, when you had to compete for oxygen with the likes of River and Savannah, it was a wonder she could find the air to giggle.

Drew suddenly appeared at my window, making the universal roll-down-your-window cranking motion. He and Catalina had followed us down in my Audi. I'd assumed only one of them would make it through the trip alive, but I caught sight of Catalina folding out too.

"What?" I snapped when I got the window down.

"We gonna camp out here or are you planning to actually drive inside?"

I glanced back at the house. I hadn't been there in years. The day I'd left, I'd sworn I'd never return. There were too many ghosts.

Lisa and I had been married for a few years when we'd renovated that house. We'd bought it as a foreclosure when the market tanked and then gutted it. We'd customized every inch of those six thousand square feet, from windows to walls, including a massive home theater over the garage. There was no way for me to walk back through those doors without seeing Lisa everywhere.

But, thanks to Cora, that part was manageable. After so many years of not even being able to utter her name, I'd smiled more than once when Cora had told a story about her old friend Lexy.

The ghosts waiting for me inside those four walls were the memories of me on my knees in our bedroom, watching her take her final breath on the screen of my phone. I remembered those twenty-nine minutes all too clearly. Lisa hadn't been in that house when she died. But I had. And I hated it because it was all I could think about after I'd lost her.

Those memories had ruined any happiness I'd felt in that house. Like how she'd decorate the whole damn thing, top to bottom, every nook and cranny, at Christmas each year. Or how, at Easter, she would force me to stay up with her all night long, stuffing a million plastic eggs with candy to hide up and down the beach for the tourists and locals alike.

No, those weren't the memories that had hit my stomach the minute that house had come into view.

Blood.

Carpet.

Screaming.

I hadn't been able to sell it though. It was all that was left of her.

But I also couldn't live there. I had caretakers who made sure it stayed clean and repairs got done on time. I'd called and given them a heads-up that we were coming into town. I think they were just as shocked by that phone call as I was.

But there I was. Cora at my side. My heart was in my throat as I sat in the driveway, unable to drive through the gate.

I looked at Drew. "Honestly, I'm not sure yet."

"Okay, well, you mind if we go inside? Cat needs to use the bathroom. I've been listening to her complain about it for the last hour."

"Oh, me too!" Savannah said, tapping on my seat. "Let me out."

"That's a great idea," Cora said, climbing out to open the back door. "All of you, go with Drew. Penn and I will be up in a few."

"Can we go down to the beach?" River asked excitedly.

None of them had ever seen the ocean. It was the only part about that trip I wasn't dreading. I got damn near giddy each time I thought about Cora's face when I took her out to the water. The girls' too.

"Wait on me for that," I answered. "There's a pool out back that you can hit up while you wait." I reached back and caught Savannah's arm before she had the chance to slide out. "Wear shorts and a tank top until we get you a bathing suit— none of that panty-and-bra shit."

She grinned, her green eyes sparkling with trouble. "Make it two bathing suits and you got a deal."

I arched an eyebrow. "One bathing suit of *my choosing*. No panty and bra shit. And twenty-four hours with no television."

Her mouth fell open. "That's not a better deal!"

"Then maybe you should stop trying to make deals with me and do what I say."

"Penn, a bathing suit of your choosing is going to be a bathrobe."

"Right? Just imagine how fly you'll look on the beach this summer."

She curled her lip. "Did you say fly? Nobody says fly anymore."

My mouth twitched as I suppressed an unlikely smile. I loved that kid. She was a pain in my ass every minute of every day. If she wasn't arguing with me or pushing my buttons, she wasn't living at all. But she was a good kid. With a good heart, and I was going to make damn sure she had a good future.

"They will when they see you in your bathrobe."

"Cora," she whined, begging for backup.

"Okay, okay, you two. Simmer down," Cora said, wading in. "*I'll* take you bathing suit shopping."

"Who says you're not going to be wearing a bathrobe too?" I asked her, my chest filling with warmth.

I loved that crazy woman too. On the drive down, we'd played a seven-hour-long game of Truth or Lie. Which for us was really a game of Truth. We swapped stories, strategically trying to stay away from the heavy stuff.

When Cora had eventually fallen asleep, River took over for her mom.

Before we'd left, Cora had made the tough decision for us to tell River about Lisa being Lexy. I'd have given anything to spare that little girl from more pain. But since we were heading to the beach house, where pictures of her were still hanging on the walls, there was no way to hide it. River had taken the news in stride, putting on a brave face and saying that she understood.

But the minute we were semi alone in that truck while everyone else slept, she laid into me with an interrogation. It was obvious she'd cared about Lisa more than I'd realized because most of her questions were disguised statements blaming me for what had happened to her. But there was no amount of blame in the world River could pin on me that I hadn't already taken on myself.

So I told her, "River, what you have to understand is I didn't *let* Lisa do anything. I was her husband. It wasn't up to me to decide how she lived her life. The only thing that role guaranteed me was the chance to live mine at her side. She knew exactly how I felt about her doing that kind of investigative work. And guess what? She did it anyway because that was important to her. You walk into a marriage thinking you can change the other person, I can promise you the only thing that is going to change is your divorce record. She was who she was. There are a lot of things that I beat myself up for on a daily basis. But how I *let* her chase her dreams is not one of them. That was never up to me."

She got quiet for a while after that, until she softly asked, "Are you going to let Cora chase her dreams too?"

I glanced at Cora while she was peacefully snoozing with her head propped against the door and replied, "No. Your mom has done enough chasing to last a lifetime. From here on out, whatever she dreams about, I'm gonna figure out a way to give it to her."

"My dad gave her the stars," River replied.

Nic Guerrero had given Cora shit, but I wasn't about to

tell his daughter that.

Instead, I shrugged, "I guess that means all there is left is the moon."

She'd smiled and then stared out the window for the next fifty miles. I knew because I'd smiled and stared in the rearview mirror at her.

Silently, I watched as all the girls got out of my truck and clambered up the driveway to the house, Drew and Catalina leading the mission.

Cora was fast to get back into the truck, and her hand came right back to mine, intertwining our fingers like she'd never left.

"You want to talk about it or just sit here for a while?" she asked.

I did not—in any way, shape, or form—deserve that woman.

But I was going to keep her for as long as she would have me.

With a sigh, I dropped my head back against the headrest and turned to face her. "This has to be weird for you. Being here. Her stuff is still in the closet, ya know? I've never done anything with this place since she died. I don't know why I brought you here. We should rent a condo or something."

She grinned. "You want me to say I'm uncomfortable so you don't have to go in there?"

She knew me too well.

Chuckling, I lifted my finger in the air and pinched them together. "A little."

"Okay. But, Penn, you slept under Nic's stars for months.

You made love to me while I was wearing his necklace. And you've taken care of his daughter without a second of hesitation. You think women's clothing in a closet is going to bother me?"

I smirked. "There's pictures too. Like one from our wedding on the mantel."

"You told me on our first date that you'd been married before. I promise I won't be shocked to see that a photographer captured still images of that momentous occasion. However, like I said, if you want me to *say* I'm uncomfortable to make you *feel* comfortable, I'm on it. But I have spent twenty hours in this truck, so I'm going to need the next place to be close by."

Laughing, I turned my gaze back onto the house. It was a nice house. A *really* nice house, right on the beach. But it hadn't been my home in years. If I was being honest, the only place I'd felt anything even remotely resembling a home was Cora's old apartment. But that had less to do with the structure and more to do with the woman and kids inside of it.

I'd grieved.

I'd moved on.

I'd met the only woman who could have ever saved me.

But pain was funny like that. It stained your soul long after you had healed.

And, being there, a part of me was waiting for that pain to reappear and consume me all over again.

But then I looked at Cora.

Her face was soft as she stared back at me.

Her lips were tipped up, gentle but teasing.

Her hair was in a messy ponytail that she'd probably yell

at me for not telling her just how messy it truly was.

How had I found something so good in the middle of something so, so bad?

Giving her hand a tug, I pulled her across the center console. I caught the back of her neck, meeting her halfway for an all-too-brief kiss, before mumbling against her lips, "I love you. And if you're comfortable being here, I'm comfortable being wherever you are."

She hummed, "Oh, my sweet Penn. Your cheesy lines are getting better. I'm impressed."

I nipped at her bottom lip. "Your jokes are not."

"So, what do you want to do? I'm really fine if you can't stay here. The girls will be crushed, Drew will bitch, and Catalina will pout." She put her hand to her chest. "But *I*, Penn Pennington, will be fine."

That was enough for me.

I laughed, putting the truck into drive.

I could do this.

I could make new memories.

Of Cora.

Of River.

Of Savannah.

Maybe even a few of Penn.

"My name is *not* Penn Pennington." I eased on the accelerator until we rolled through the gate.

She laughed, loud and carefree.

And after we'd parked, climbed the back steps, and then walked through the door together, those twenty-nine minutes of memories didn't assault me.

Not with her smiling up at me.

"Oh my God! Did you feel that?" she cried, wiggling in my arms when another wave crashed into us. Her legs were wrapped around my hips, two scraps of fabric dividing us, my cock painfully hard. But as River and Isabel chased Savannah across the beach with a piece of wet sea grass, there was not the first damn thing I could do about it.

"You had to buy a fucking bikini, didn't you?" I grumbled for no less than the twentieth time since we'd gotten back from the beach shop.

"Could you stop worrying about what I'm wearing and more about the shark who is about to tear my legs off?"

"What shark?" I reached behind me and tickled the bottom of her foot.

She screamed at the top of her lungs, fighting to get away, but I refused to let her go.

Turns out, Cora couldn't swim.

Neither could River.

Or Savannah.

Having grown up on the water, where people taught their babies to swim before they could talk, I'd never considered they wouldn't know how.

But I'd guessed, in Chicago, it wasn't as imperative.

"That was not funny," she scolded.

"Oh, come on. It was a little funny."

She swung her head from one side to the other. "Why can't I see the bottom? Aren't you supposed to see the bottom?"

I barked a laugh, sliding my hands down to cup her ass. "Maybe if we were in the Keys."

"Okay, so let's go there. This place is scary."

I spun in a fast circle, the sand tunneling beneath my feet, Cora clinging to my neck. "It's a two-hour drive, baby."

"Penn, stop!"

She had hated every minute of it since I'd dragged her into the water.

Every shell she stepped on was a crab and every swish of the water was a jellyfish.

I'd held her captive out there for a full thirty minutes, laughing the whole time.

It never got old. However, it was becoming blatantly clear that a life on the beach was not in our future. Maybe a winter home where we could escape the cold and she could sit on the deck, sipping a cup of coffee, and watching the waves roll in.

But if not Chicago.

And not Florida.

Where?

"Where do you want to live?" I asked, heading back to the shallow waters.

She continued searching the murky water for the invisible shark. "What do you mean?"

"When this is all over, Thomas and Manuel are either sharing a cell or a grave, and we finally get to start a life together, where do you want to live?"

Her eyebrows drew together as her gaze bounced to mine. "What are my choices?"

"Ummm...planet Earth. I've got money, but not Mars

money. And at the rate I've been going, I won't even have Earth money in a few years, so I'll probably need to find a job at some point, so let's attempt to keep it somewhere with English as the first language."

When we reached waist-level—for her—I set her on her feet.

She cringed when her toes hit the sand, but if I had any hope of deflating my hard-on in the next, oh, million years, I needed to stop her from rubbing against it with every step. I dropped to my knees so as not to scandalize the public beach.

"You good?" I asked.

She straightened her back. "Yeah. I could probably run from a shark if he got any ideas. This feels more solid than liquid here."

Underwater, I clamped my hand down on her calf and she jumped straight in the air, letting out an ear-piercing shriek.

I roared with laughter and she splashed water in my face. "Dammit, Penn."

"Okay. Okay. Okay." I lifted my hands in surrender. "I promise: no more fucking with you." I rose to my feet when the stretch of my swim trunks told me it was safe and tossed my arm around her shoulders. "So, seriously, where do you want to live?"

She reached up, caught my hand dangling over her shoulder, and laced our fingers. Together, we started toward the shore. Catalina and Drew were chilling with beers under an umbrella. Oh, so casual for a man on a suicide mission and a shattered woman with a taste for psychological warfare.

"I don't know," Cora said. "Cat and I had talked about

Seattle when I finished my degree."

My eyebrows popped up. Seattle was amazing, but it didn't strike me as Cora's scene. Then again, I wasn't sure what her scene was. She'd always been such a homebody by necessity.

I abruptly stopped walking, pulling her up short with me. "Seattle?"

She shrugged. "There's a lot of coffee there. It's like my personal Bat-Signal."

"There's coffee everywhere, babe. Not sure that should be your only prerequisite for where you settle. But if Seattle is what you want, I'm down." I slanted my head when a thought donned on me. "Wait... Do you want to get married?"

Her whole body jolted, including her eyes, which flashed comically wide.

"Wait. Wait. Wait. That wasn't a proposal," I clarified. "I'm not asking if *you* want to marry *me*."

The only thing more humorous than her wide eyes was her palpable disappointment.

My chest didn't just warm. It ignited in an all-out wildfire. And not like the one that had been roaring inside me for the last four years. This one was a controlled burn, destroying all the debris, creating room for new growth.

She wanted to be with me.

And fuck me, but I wanted to be with her more than I'd wanted anything in my entire life: Cora, food, water, shelter. In that order.

But I didn't need a marriage certificate or a ring on her finger to make that come to fruition.

I just needed her.

Curling her into my side, I kissed the top of her head. "Relax. I'm not asking *yet*, okay? It occurred to me that we've spent so much time discussing the past that I never found out what you want out of life. We've talked about you finishing college and getting your degree, but what next? Would you want to get married in general? Not just to me."

She gave me the side-eye. "I'm not down with polygamy, Penn Pennington."

I laughed.

Craning her head back, she peered up into my eyes. "Yeah. I'd get married again." She nudged me with her elbow. "Assuming the right guy asked."

I grinned down at her and started walking again. "You want kids?"

She buzzed her lips. "Wow. I honestly don't know. I never thought I'd have the option again." Her nose crinkled and she swayed her head from side to side in consideration. "I love kids, but with the way things went the first time, I'd have to feel...*safe* before taking that leap again."

Safe. Kids or not. I could give that to her.

I *would* give that to her. I could give her the most boring, uneventful, simple life in the world. Not usually a selling point for a marriage, but for us, the slow life was exactly what we finally needed.

"You?" she asked, her voice squeaking at the end like she was preparing for the answer.

"I'd love to start a family. Lisa was never interested. It didn't fit into her lifestyle. I accepted that. But if it were up to me, I'd want a couple."

"Really?" she whispered.

I nudged her the way she'd done me. "Assuming the right woman said yes."

Her feet kept moving, but she melted into my side, making me think maybe she'd made her decision on kids too.

"Boys or girls?" she asked.

"Boys. I think getting Savannah and River to adulthood is going to be enough to do my head in."

"Aww." She flashed me a smile. "Thank you for always including them. From day one. I can't tell you how much that means to me."

"You don't need to thank me for that, Cora. Spending time with them has not been a hardship."

"For other men, it would be."

I shot her a wink. "Then let's hope none of those *other men* propose before I do."

Her cheeks pinked and she turned her attention down to her sandy feet, muttering, "Fingers crossed."

As we got closer to Drew and Catalina, I squinted, trying to force my brain to make sense of what I was seeing. He was lying on his side, facing her, sporting a huge grin while drizzling wet sand into the palm of her hand. She was laughing, her dark hair blowing in the wind as she sat with her legs stretched out beside him, in a bikini much like Cora's.

And though they were both wearing shades, it was beyond obvious that there was some serious eye-fucking being exchanged, at least on Drew's side.

I had no idea what had happened in my Audi on that twenty-hour car ride from Chicago. But if the nightmare in front of me was any indication, the engine exhaust had to have been rerouted into the car and affected both of their brains.

"Hey," Catalina chirped, jerking her hand away when she tore her eyes off Drew long enough to realize that other people existed.

Fuck. I didn't want to imagine the epic clusterfuck that would ensue if those two started something.

Drew was a good guy, and while wooing women was definitely his thing, staying with them was *not*.

"Hey," I replied gruffly, shooting him a silent what-the-fuck-are-you-doing glare.

It sailed right over his head. "Hey, so, how do you feel about me and Cat taking the girls out to a movie tonight?"

"I don't. And it's not happening," I muttered, releasing Cora to grab two beers from the cooler. I twisted the top off one, passed it her way, and then did the same on mine.

"And why not?" he asked defensively.

I sat on the top of the cooler, patting my thigh in an invitation Cora quickly accepted. As she settled on my lap, I replied, "Because this isn't a vacation. I have no idea what Thomas and Manuel are up to right now, but it's better for all of us if we stay tight, keep our heads up, and try to figure out what's next."

"Right," he mumbled in a way that sounded more like *fuck you* than it did an agreement.

"Oh, I know!" Catalina exclaimed. "What if we rent a movie and watch it in that theater room over the garage?" She waggled her eyebrows. "Maybe give you two some time alone in the house."

Now, that I could get on board with. If it bought me

some much-needed alone time with Cora, Drew and Catalina could eye-fuck all damn night.

"What movie?" Cora asked.

I grazed my teeth over her shoulder. "It doesn't matter. You're not watching it."

Drew grinned and then pushed his sunglasses down his nose, narrowing his gaze on Cora's feet. "Holy shit, is that a sand shark?"

And that was how I became deaf.

She flew straight up into the air, but not before screaming in my ear. I nearly dropped my beer, and hers spilled all over us both. But Drew and Catalina laughed so hard that it almost made it worth it.

"Baby, chill." I chuckled, dragging her back down onto my lap. "Sand sharks still live in the ocean."

"Oh my God! I hate you people—all of you."

"Hey, what did I do?" Catalina whined.

"You're laughing," she spat.

And she was.

And so was Drew.

And then I joined the group.

And it wasn't but a few seconds later that Cora joined us too.

As it would seem we were one big, happy family.

It wasn't until a few hours later, as a river of blood forged a path across my living room floor, that I realized it had all been one big fucking *lie*.

CHAPTER NINETEEN

Cora

'd lied. Staying at Lisa's house was a little weird.

After we got back from the beach, everyone scattered to the various bathrooms across the house—all five of them.

My hair was still wet as I padded through the maze of wood floors in search of my man. "Penn?" I called.

"Right here, baby."

I followed his voice to the end of a different hallway and found him staring at a closed door to what had to have been the master bedroom. He'd avoided it like the plague on the grand tour earlier. And while the bedroom Penn had dropped our bags in was large with a private bath, there was no way that it was the master in a place that luxurious.

"What are you doing?" I asked. I wasn't too proud to admit that a pang of jealousy hit me when I imagined what he was thinking about.

All the nights he'd made love to her in that room.

All the nights she'd fallen asleep at his side.

All the mornings he'd kissed her goodbye before going out for his run.

He'd loved her. And that was okay. But that didn't mean I enjoyed thinking about them together, which was proving to be a teensy bit difficult because there was way more than just a wedding picture on the mantel. Before we'd gone down to the beach, Penn had removed the majority of them. And he'd done it smiling and not in agonizing pain, the way I'd expected after his mini panic attack in the truck.

But she was still there in that house with us.

And I hated the idea that maybe he was lost in his memories with her.

His blue eyes came to mine, the weight of his gaze stealing my breath. "Debating if I can ever go in there again."

I swallowed hard. "It's just walls and memories. She's not behind that door."

"No. But I am. That night, when I watched her die, I was in that room. And for twenty-nine minutes, Thomas Lyons and those men killed me too. In some ways, it feels like a blurry, distant memory. In others, it's so sharp and fresh I can see it on the back of my lids."

God, I was an ass. While I was busy getting jealous of a woman who was no longer alive, Penn was lost in the bad times, not the good.

"Oh, Penn," I breathed, hurrying over to wrap him in a hug. "I'm so sorry."

He put his lips to the top of my head and inhaled deeply. "I think she would have liked this."

I put my chin to his chest and looked up at him. "Liked what?"

"Me and you."

I smiled. "You were her husband. I can speak with absolute certainty when I say she would have *hated* your new girlfriend."

He grinned, taking aim at my mouth for a quick peck. "I'm not one of those people who believe that everything happens for a reason. I'll never be able to say that there was a reason why she should have died." He kissed me again, letting it linger as he drew in a reverent breath. "But maybe you're why I had to watch."

Chills exploded across my skin, and my nose started stinging. "No, baby. No. That was—"

"The only reason I got you," he finished. "Experiencing that anger, and pain, and helplessness, it lit the fire, Cora. And it burned hotter every day until I met you. Losing her would have brought me to my knees no matter what. But watching it happen made sure I could never get back up. It set everything in motion. It birthed the rage that demanded vengeance. And then that same vengeance guided me straight to your door."

My heart hurt. I did not want to be the silver lining to his nightmare. He'd always see that in me, and I wanted to be something different for Penn. Something *good*.

"I don't know about that, Penn. Drew didn't watch and he seems to have that same rage brewing inside him."

His brow furrowed as confusion hit his face. "Drew?" He paused. "Did I ever tell you where he was the night Lisa died?"

I shook my head, an odd sense of unease taking up root in my stomach.

He briefly closed his eyes. "A half a mile away from her."

213

I jolted like his arms had become electrified. "What? I thought—"

"Drew and I got the worst of both worlds. I had to watch from over a thousand miles away, while he was sitting at the bar just down the street, waiting for her to show up, clueless that she was dying only blocks away."

The breath tore from my throat like he'd punched me. "How?"

"He *hated* when she went out on those assignments like that. Drew's way of handling that fear was by pretending it wasn't happening, so he dodged her calls for over a month. They were always super close and it was bothering her that he wouldn't answer. So, one night, he and I went out for a drink and I gave him so much shit that he finally relented. He called her, and she told him all about the Guerreros, and Thomas, and *you*. Which, for Drew, knowing everything only made it worse. So, a couple days later, he got on a plane, flew up there, bound and determined to drag her home. And if anyone could do it, it was her brother."

He smiled, tight and sad. "I was so fucking thrilled I bought the plane ticket myself. She was pissed when she found out he was there, refused to tell him where she was staying—probably because it was your building on that particular night—but she told him to meet her at the bar the following night. She never showed up though."

My vision swam as memories of him running to me at the group home after he'd heard Thomas mention his sister. I'd thought he was pissed, but only then did I understand the fear that had ghosted across his face. My stomach twisted in knots. "Oh my God. Poor Drew. He was so close."

Penn nodded painfully. "Yeah. He was the only reason the cops found her at all. He'd mentioned the name of the bar to me in passing, and when I *finally* remembered it, I told the nine-one-one operator and they sent cars to both of the nearby hotels. So when I tell you that Drew has that same rage inside him. I mean, he has the *same. Fucking. Rage.*"

"Oh, God. You should have told me that before I started poking his eye. He couldn't save his sister and I've been giving him a scar of my fingerprint."

Penn grinned. "Don't worry about it. He'll eventually give you a reason to feel good about it again."

Gliding my fingers up the nape of his neck, I pushed up onto my toes and brushed my lips over his, offering the only comfort I could. "I'm so sorry you guys had to deal with all that."

"Me too. But standing here with you right now makes that room a whole hell of a lot less scary."

My stomach fluttered. Okay, so maybe being the silver lining to Penn's nightmare wasn't so bad after all. At least he had one now.

Shifting his weight back and forth, he rocked me in his arms. "Would it be weird if I asked you to go in there with me?"

My lips hitched. "Yes. Totally weird. But if you're asking if I will, then yes. Absolutely."

He kissed me, this time opening his mouth, his tongue sweeping mine. It was sensual, but it wasn't sexual. It was sweet and filled with gratitude. It was Penn's way of saying thank you without the use of words.

And even though I didn't need thanks for loving him,

I took whatever he was willing to give, losing myself in the beauty of something so simple.

But when the sound of a woman's scream echoed through the hall, I realized that nothing in our life would ever be simple.

CHAPTER TWENTY

Cora

My body came alive in the next second, adrenaline surging through my veins like a tsunami.

"Stay here," Penn growled, sprinting away and leaving me alone in the hallway, Catalina's voice still echoing in my ears.

It was the kind of scream that made people act first and think second because there was no mistaking it for anything except terror. And, because of that, I did *not* heed Penn's instructions, but rather took off after him.

As I ran, I scanned my head for memories of where the girls were. Last I'd seen of them, they were heading out to the theater room above the garage. I had no idea what was happening, but I felt a morsel of relief knowing they weren't in the main house.

When I rounded the corner into the living room, I nearly plowed into Penn. He was frozen at the mouth of the hall, his chest heaving, but it had nothing to do with the short run.

It had been years since I'd seen his face, but it still sent a chill down my spine.

Marcos's dark hair.

Dante's malevolent stare.

Nic's strong jaw.

Manuel Guerrero. The patriarch of the Guerrero clan. The man who had taken my child, manipulated me, and imprisoned me in his world for over a decade. And he was currently standing in Penn's living room, his arm around his daughter's throat, with the tip of a gun digging into her temple.

"You son of a bitch," Penn growled, lunging forward.

He scrambled back with clumsy movements, the gun shaking in his hand as he dragged Catalina with him. "Back the fuck up. I will put a fucking bullet in her head right this fucking second."

"You better know how to run. Anything happens to her and you are three seconds behind her on the way to the other side."

Manuel laughed, gruff and throaty, and it tangibly slithered over my skin. "I'm a dead man already, you fucking fool!"

I held my breath as his finger teetered entirely too close to the trigger.

Grabbing Penn's arm, I tried to pull him back while pleading, "Please, stop. You're making it worse."

He shook me off, snarling without ever tearing his gaze off Manuel. "Get the fuck out of here, Cor."

With my heart in my throat, I looked at Catalina.

Her eyes were wide, aimed right back at me. "*Go*," she mouthed.

I shook my head, panic building in my chest. There had to be a way out.

There *had* to be a solution where this finally ended once

and for all.

I was so damn done with the constant pendulum of emotions.

One minute, I was kissing in the clouds with Penn.

The next, the king of demons had arrived.

Something had to give.

I just had no clue what that was going to be, and I was hoping that it wasn't Catalina's life.

I folded my hands together in prayer. "Manny, please. Don't do this. She's the only family you have left."

His face got hard, and his thick, furry eyebrows pinched together. "And whose fucking fault is that? It wasn't enough you took Nic from me. You had to come after Marcos and Dante too?"

I stiffened, praying to any and every god that would listen that he didn't know that Penn was responsible for that. There was no arguing with him about Nic. I'd been guilty in his eyes since day one. But if I could keep him talking, his anger focused on me, maybe Catalina could make a move. He was older and overweight. If it weren't for the gun at her head, she could have easily gotten away from him. And then Penn, who was fuming at my side, could have subdued him—and more than likely killed him.

But we needed that window, a moment of distraction.

Keeping my voice even and calm so as not to match his intensity, I half lied, "I had nothing to do with the fire. Neither did Cat. So just let her go."

"You've been a curse on everyone you have touched your entire life. My sons, his brother, and now, you've sunk your teeth into his brother-in-law. No wonder Drew was so fast to tell me where you were."

The air in the room stilled.

The proverbial record stopping.

What. The. Fuck.

Out of the corner of my eye, I saw Penn jerk.

But I stared at Manuel, trying to make heads or tails.

Drew?

Drew had told him where we were?

Where the hell was Drew?

Manuel continued his rant. "You're a fucking black widow. Medusa in disguise." Suddenly, his gun swung my way. "I should have fucking gutted you the day you killed Nic."

My pulse soared as chaos broke out. Penn jumped in front of me, tucking me into his back, yelling at Manuel.

But before I lost sight of Catalina, I noticed something.

She wasn't fighting.

Her eyes were big, tears were streaming down her face, but she didn't try to get away.

That should have been her moment. His arm around her neck loosened as the gun came away from her head. And she just stood there.

"Cora," Penn growled. "Get the fuck out of here. *Now.*"

My life had never been great. Not until recently, anyway, and even then, it had decidedly not been easy.

But with Penn back, talking about Seattle, babies, and wedding rings, it was getting there.

However, right then, as Drew came walking around the corner, his hands in the air, Thomas's gun at his back, I started thinking that Manuel was right.

Maybe I was a curse.

Penn

"No. No. Please stay, Cora," Thomas crooned, strolling into the living room with a gun at Drew's back.

Molten lava replaced the blood in my veins.

What the fucking fuck was going on?

No goddamn way Drew told Manuel where we were. Yes, they'd been buddies in prison, but none of that had been real. He was my brother despite our birth certificates listing different parents. From day one, he and I had been in this together. Every step. Every breath. Every minute of every day, we'd shared the same ravenous thirst for revenge.

The Earth being flat was more believable than him flipping on me.

But what the fuck was he playing at, and why had he kept me in the dark?

Catalina struggled in her father's arms when she saw her ex-husband.

"Honey, I'm home," he singsonged with a wide smile.

Backing up, I forced Cora closer behind me and attempted to catch my brother's gaze.

His eyes were locked on Catalina's though.

"Now, would you look at this," Thomas said cheerfully. "It's a family reunion. Well, minus our dear friend Lisa." He tipped his head my way. "My sincerest condolences. She was a lovely woman. But, as she learned, I am not a man to be challenged. I gave her every opportunity to get out of my city, Shane. I swear I did. Personally, I admired her tenacity, right up until the moment I ordered them to slit her throat." He grinned.

My vision flashed red, and I ground my teeth. It would have been all too easy to allow that pent-up rage bubbling to the surface to overtake me. But it would have left Cora exposed, and that was not a risk I could afford to take with her, not even if it finally gave me the satisfaction of ripping Thomas Lyons's head from his shoulders.

It was a true testament to my self-control when I didn't move a muscle.

He leaned to the side, attempting to catch a glance at Cora, but I shifted so he couldn't see her.

I didn't even want his gaze to touch her.

He arrogantly cocked his head. "Did your wife know you have a taste for whores, or is this a new predilection of yours?"

My entire body strained, swelling until I feared that it would rip free of my skin. My hands ached, and the same burning Cora had tamed within me was back and thrumming with need to—

"Enough," Drew growled, joining the conversation.

My gaze jumped to him, searching for a clue—any fucking clue—to what was truly going on, but his face was an empty and emotionless pit.

He shoved at Thomas's arm. "Get that fucking gun out of my face. I did it, okay? You want Catalina? There she is. But this is done—do you understand me? You forget about me. Both of you. I want no fucking part of this anymore." He planted his hands on his hips and stared at the floor. "I'm sorry, Shane. But I can't live like this. It's not worth this shit. I gotta get out of this life. The running, the hiding. The constant looking over my shoulder. I might as well go back to prison if that's how I've gotta live my life. I just want it over. I need it *over*."

And then he finally looked up at me, his dark gaze hitting mine with all the gentleness of a sledgehammer.

Oh, yes. I knew Drew Walker.

We'd met in college at MIT. He was two years younger than I was, studying mechanical engineering. The kid was so fucking smart that, in the five years it took me to graduate, he'd caught up and we'd walked across that stage together. He was livid when he'd found me in bed with his sister and refused to speak to me for a whopping six days. But when we graduated and I moved her back to Florida, he bought a house two blocks away. And on the day I slid a ring on her finger, vowing until death do us part, he'd been not only my best man but also her man of honor.

Drew Walker was sewn into the fabric of my life.

I would never for the rest of my life forget the look on his face the night we shook on our commitment to find and kill the man responsible for Lisa's death.

As I held his gaze from across the room now, it was that same ruthless determination staring back at me—and this time, he really was done.

The hairs on my arms stood on end and my chest caved in on me, but before I could utter a single syllable, Drew spun, pulled a knife from the back of his pants, and, in one fluid movement, carved a horseshoe across Thomas's neck.

Blood exploded from his skin. Shock registered on his face, and his hands went up to his throat as though he could stop it.

I wanted to gawk as he fell to his knees, relishing in his pain.

I wanted to watch the crimson blood seep from his throat as he coughed and gurgled, unsure if he would drown or bleed to death first.

I wanted to squat in front of him and stare into his eyes as the life slipped from his eyes.

I wanted twenty-nine minutes to make him suffer.

But I was willing to settle for twenty-nine seconds of watching him die.

Unfortunately, I couldn't have either.

Cora was there, her sweet, soft body trembling at my back. And I was more concerned with Manuel's reaction and the bullets that were about to soar through the air than I was basking in revenge.

I swung my gaze to Manuel. Waiting and ready for my window to take him down.

Manuel was smiling wide though. "Jesus Christ, Walker, could that have possibly taken you any longer?"

Drew replied, "Do not fucking start with me, old man. I have no patience with your bullshit. You showed up fifteen fucking minutes early. I barely got back from dropping the kids off at the movies in time. I told your ass last night to be here at eight." Cool, casual Drew turned his eyes my way. "Oh, hey, Shane. FYI, I took the kids to the movies. I know you said you didn't want them out of sight, but I didn't want them here for this."

I blinked and then rumbled, "And what the fuck is *this*, exactly?"

Catalina caught my attention as she stepped away from her father. "Cora, you okay?"

"Um…no. No, like no…nothing. I have no idea," she

rambled, remaining tight at my back.

Wiping the handle of the knife on his shirt, Drew walked over to Manuel and then traded him weapons.

"Perhaps, next time, you can get me a fucking gun that actually has bullets," Manuel grumbled.

"Never trust a felon, Manny. I believe you were the one who taught me that." Drew winked, curling Catalina into his front.

I just stood there blinking, my head pounding as I tried to figure out what the hell was happening.

"What is going on?" Cora whispered.

I had no fucking idea.

Blood was everywhere.

Thomas was keeled over to the side, facedown in a puddle.

Manuel groaned with pain as he walked to the couch and sat down, breathing like he'd run a marathon, not walked six steps.

And Drew—well, he was peppering kisses on the top of Catalina's head like they were long-lost loves and not standing next to the body of her husband.

"Catalina, honey," Manuel called. "I don't want to see that shit. I spent the last twenty-four hours with that prick. I'm tired. Get on the phone and call the police and let them know that your father just killed your husband."

What the damn shit fucking hell was going on!

CHAPTER TWENTY-ONE

Drew

I should probably start at the beginning.

So there we were, two of my fingers buried in her tight pussy. Her round tits and dark nipples were swaying as she arched her back off the black leather seat of my rental.

Okay, wait, that's not really the beginning. But those were the parts that made my cock twitch the minute she opened the door that day Cora, River, and I had arrived at her house.

The beginning would really be that same night, four years earlier, when she walked into the bar. I tagged her immediately. Honestly, I think every person in the bar did. And not because she was gorgeous—which she fucking was. But rather because the bar was a filthy little hole in the wall and she strutted in looking like a senator's wife.

She was wearing a black knee-length skirt that clung to her ass in all the right ways and a cream silk top that bordered on the line between sexy librarian and eighty-year-old grandmother. But, with a chest like hers, it was leaning heavily toward librarian. Her long, toned legs were capped by black pumps, and her fingers were perfectly manicured with white tips. But, even without all of that, her plump lips had been enough to command my attention.

I watched her for the first hour as she toyed with the ends of her long, brown hair. She downed three martinis while alternating between nervously checking her phone and staring at the door.

The second hour, I decided to make an approach while silently declaring that whichever douchebag was stupid enough to invite a woman like that to a place like *that* and then stand her up was my new favorite dumbass in the world.

I'd been going stir-crazy while sitting in the hotel, but I had a few more hours to kill before Lisa was supposed to meet me there. And what better way to kill time than with a beautiful woman.

I hadn't said hello before she scooted down two stools.

I'd given her space, but only physically.

I started conversations, and just as quickly, she shut them down.

But then it only became a challenge to me, and considering that talking was my forte, it wasn't but about thirty minutes before I cracked her.

Well, almost cracked her. "Leave me the fuck alone" was still talking.

She'd told me that she was waiting for a friend. And every time the door to that bar opened, I prayed like hell that friend did *not* come through it.

It took me a little while, but eventually, I got her talking— two more martinis aided me in that task.

And then I was fucking done for.

She was so damn funny—a real ball-buster. I loved every minute of her snarky retorts and teasing side-eyes. I swear to

God I laughed more with that woman over the span of the next three hours than I had in my entire life.

And when she started looking through her phone for the number of a cab company, the thought of her leaving hit me far deeper than it should have.

I asked her to stay.

She told me no.

I asked her to let me drive her home.

She told me no.

I asked her to come back to my hotel room.

She told me no.

I asked her for her number.

She told me...*no.*

But, as we waited together outside in the dark parking lot, I didn't ask before I dipped my head and took her mouth in a kiss that changed my entire life.

Because it happened at the exact moment I *failed* the only woman in my life who mattered.

We watched her cab come and leave, laughing and making out like high schoolers in the front seat before moving to the back.

Penn was blowing up my phone the entire time I was inside her.

And when I finally picked up, I kicked her out of my car so fast that I didn't even remember if she was dressed.

Her name was Cat and she was the biggest regret of my life.

I'd never been brave enough to admit that I was a thirty-one-year-old man fucking a random woman in the back of my car the night my sister was murdered half a mile away from me—not even to Penn.

Somewhere in my self-loathing and desperate need to place blame for what had happened, it'd all become her fault.

She was gorgeous, funny, and smart—the perfect storm of a woman the devil himself must have planted in that bar to distract me.

I didn't know what hotel Lisa was staying at, but in the What-if game, rationale didn't matter.

If Cat hadn't been there, maybe I would have left earlier.

Maybe I would have driven past the hotel and seen a commotion.

Maybe in those twenty-nine fucking minutes, I could have found her and saved her.

But no, I'd been fucking a woman named Cat while my sister was being beaten, tortured, and stabbed.

Fucking Cat.

So imagine my surprise when, some months later, I started digging into the Guerrero family and her face popped up in the private investigator's findings.

She was married. Had been for way longer than four years. And she and her daughter had gone missing. Presumably dead. But it seemed all too convenient to me that she was there with me that night. It solidified my suspicions that the Guerreros were involved. That was the moment I volunteered to go to prison. My life was over, and I lost my job after I'd become so wrapped up in my own pain that I stopped showing up. I'd eventually run out of money. The only thing I'd be losing was Shane. And he was a fucking mess. Every time he looked at me, I thought he could see what I'd done until I started avoiding him altogether.

But then I'd miss Lisa, and he was all that was left of her.

Two years in a cell with Manuel Guerrero and the only info I'd truly gotten was that the same woman who I irrationally hated more than anyone else in the world was the woman I had to find in order to finally escape the pain altogether.

I'd hoped she wouldn't recognize me when Cora had given me directions to her house that day. It had been four years, so maybe I'd ghosted from her memories the way I'd never been able to get rid of her.

One glance and I was back in that bar. Catalina was still beautiful.

But her eyes weren't the same.

Or maybe it was *my eyes.*

I knew more about her now. Like why she was on the run. How she had gotten her daughter. And who her husband was. And then other things, like how she was the only person who had ever been good to Cora. And God knew I'd fallen head over heels in love with that woman. Not in the sense that Shane loved her of course, but there wasn't anything I wouldn't do for her or those kids.

So when Catalina cornered me in her house that first night, demanding to know who the hell I was and what the hell I was up to, my misplaced hate for her melted away.

I kissed her.

She slapped me.

And then, hours later when she heard Thomas's gunshot from the bedroom I'd put them in before opening the front door, she screamed my name in such a terrified tone that I'd never be able to erase the imprint it made on my soul.

When Shane had told me that he'd found her in the hall,

being choked by a man I didn't even know was in the house at the time, the weight of failure took out my knees.

Cat and I did not see eye to eye on damn near anything, but there was something about that smart-ass woman. And when she snuck into my bedroom early that morning in Shane's apartment in Chicago, while he was sleeping on the couch and Cora was in with River and Savannah, we finally got the chance to talk.

And I told her the truth. All of it.

But I didn't want her truths, because while I thought she was beautiful and incredible, her truths bound us together in ways that made me wish for lies.

She'd been at the bar that night to meet Lisa at seven.

I was supposed to meet her at nine.

My fucking Sherlock Holmes of a sister had been following Catalina and begging her to help take Thomas down. Seriously, my sister was crazytown.

But, apparently, it'd worked, because in Catalina's purse that night had been all the necessary documentation she was planning to turn over.

And I'd fucked her.

While Lisa was dying and Catalina's life at home was terrifying, I'd fucked her in the back seat of a car like a whore.

She told me that, at that time when she was taking the first steps to reclaim her life and figuring out who she was as a woman, the fact that someone genuinely wanted her and was kind and gentle about it had been the biggest turn-on of her life.

She'd also told me that, when I'd kicked her out of the car half-naked and alone in an empty parking lot for reasons that

I had not explained, I'd changed her life too.

And not for the better.

She'd gone home dejected and feeling more used than ever, and she'd caved to Thomas's demands to testify against her father. And then spent four years living in solitude with Isabel, for fear of ever taking another chance on a man.

Much to my surprise, she let me hold her that night in Shane's bed. And when we woke to him and Cora arguing in the kitchen, she slipped back out of my life for what I feared was the very last time.

That is until Manuel called my phone later that morning while we were cooking eggs and bacon for the girls, before the news of his escape had even hit the local news.

Despite the fact that he had agreed to help Thomas track down Catalina in exchange for his freedom, the only thing Manuel truly wanted was Thomas dead. And he wanted me to do it.

That I could do.

That I could so fucking do.

Manuel had no delusions about the fact that he was going back to jail. He was dying, and he said that he could go peacefully as long as Thomas Lyons made it to hell before he did.

And then he shocked the shit out of me by telling me exactly where Catalina had been in hiding and asked me to go get her so he could see her one last time before he died. It seemed losing three of your four children and preparing to meet our maker softened the man.

And considering she was standing right next to me, tears rolling down her face at the knowledge that he'd known where she had been all along and never turned her over to Thomas or Marcos or Dante, she picked up the phone. They talked for over an hour. And while I'd say that chat was therapeutic for Catalina, nothing was forgotten during that conversation. She hated him. But she finally got some closure.

When the three of us hatched the plan to come down to Florida—neutral territory so Thomas couldn't get squirrelly and pull any bullshit on us—I decided to supply the weapons—filled with blanks.

Rightly so, Thomas decided he didn't trust me at the last minute. When he and Manuel showed up to reclaim and kill Thomas's wife, he confiscated my gun. But that was okay—my plan had always been to drain that motherfucker.

And right then, as I lifted Catalina into my arms across the room from her abusive husband's dead body, with Manuel on his way back to prison where he belonged and Penn and Cora huddled together, offering each other love and reassurance, I finally felt the overwhelming weight of losing Lisa fall from my shoulders.

It was done.

It was finally fucking done.

CHAPTER TWENTY-TWO

Penn

Another fucking hotel.

Though this one was a two-bedroom beachfront suite and I'd never been so excited in my entire fucking life.

She was there.

They were there.

And, soon, I'd be there with them.

Forever.

Earlier in the night, Manuel had sat on *my* couch, sipping a bottle of *my* water, and glared daggers at *my* woman as Catalina and Drew had given us the who, what, when, where, and how of what had gone down. After everything Manuel had put Cora through, it took all of the self-restraint I possessed not to leave him on the floor beside Thomas. Or, at the very least, tell him that I was Penn Walker and then give him the play-by-play including every excruciating detail about how I'd killed his sons. The *only* thing that had stopped me was the fact that Manuel was taking the fall for the dead man in my living room and not Drew.

Per Drew's stupid-ass plan, Cora had taken the truck

and left before Catalina called the cops.

There was no reason for her to be involved in any of this. With her record and the fact that we were harboring a teenage runaway, it was best for everyone involved if she picked up all the kids from the theater and took them somewhere safe. Cora had dropped Isabel off a few streets up, and just as the cops had arrived she'd come running up the beach and into her mother's arms.

The cops had been at my house for hours, asking questions, taking pictures, and searching the place. I had to admit Drew had covered his bases.

The lies we'd all agreed on went like this: Lisa was left out completely. Catalina and Drew had started dating after he'd been sent by his old prison buddy to find his daughter. She was hiding from her husband and brothers and she didn't trust law enforcement. So her new boyfriend, Drew, had brought her down to my house—the only place he'd thought he could make her safe.

Thomas and Manuel had tracked them down.

Manuel had thought they were saving Catalina, and Thomas had double-crossed him and tried to kill her. Manuel got there first, with a knife to Thomas's throat.

The end.

With Manuel's capture and confession, there wasn't a lot of whodunit police work happening. The whys, though, were definitely in play, especially when they realized that Catalina and her daughter had been declared missing persons for four years.

But, like she'd promised, she had more than enough dirt on Thomas to put him away for life. In this case, it was shared after his life had ended, but it was useful nonetheless. All of her allegations were corroborated with a small filing cabinet she'd instructed the police how to find in a storage unit in Wisconsin. In it were countless documents tying Thomas to Guerrero business and videos of him assaulting her and Isabel.

I was the first to be released from police questioning. After all, I was just the innocent, clueless brother-in-law with no motive.

Catalina, Isabel, and Drew were still at the police station, but they had attorneys, and when I'd caught sight of Drew as I'd left, he was smiling in a semicircle with a few cops.

It was good that he was making some friends in uniform, because the moment I saw him, I was going to beat the ever-loving shit out of him. He needed all the protection he could get. That dumbass had told me nothing of his little plan. He'd said that he was too afraid I'd tell Cora, who no doubt would have thrown the brakes on some stupid shit like that.

And, given our new honesty policy, he would have been right, I absolutely would have told her—and then *I* would have thrown the brakes on some stupid shit like that.

But it had worked.

Thomas was dead.

Manuel was back behind bars.

And I was walking into a fucking hotel room, where my woman and kids were waiting on me.

I knocked softly, and it took her less than a second to open the door. I'd called to tell her that I was on the way up, but I would have much preferred a "who is it" before she pulled it wide.

"Baby, did you even check the peephole?"

She didn't reply as she threw her arms around my hips, brought her torso flush against me, and then smooshed her face against my chest.

I smiled, smoothing down the back of her hair. "You okay?"

She shook her head.

I walked into the room with her still plastered to my front; my every step forward she matched with one back. "You want to lay down and talk about it?"

The door clicking shut behind us was the only sound in the otherwise silent suite.

She craned her head back, her red-rimmed eyes meeting mine. I hated that she'd spent the rest of the night crying, but the reasons for those tears were fine by me.

"It was too easy," she whispered.

My eyebrows shot up. "Easy? Are you kidding me? I think I've died at least seventeen times tonight alone."

"Something is going to happen, Penn. I just feel it."

I scooped her off her feet and carried her to the bedroom, though I paused at a cracked door with one brown eye and one green eye peering out at us. I wanted to check on them, give them a once-over, to reassure them and my own frazzled mind that we'd all made it out unscathed. But, when I shot them a wink, I heard a giggle and then the door quickly shut.

When we got to our room, the bed was unmade like she'd not only been in it already but spent that time tossing and turning rather than resting. I set her on the edge, toed my shoes off, and then crawled in. My overstressed body sagged into the cool, soft sheets. Cora did not delay in assuming her spot at my side, her leg across my hips, her head on my shoulder, and her hand on my chest.

"You're right," I told her as soon as we both got comfortable. "Something is going to happen. We're gonna buy a house in Seattle. I'm going to put a ring on your finger. God willing, a baby in your belly. Savannah is gonna get a homeschool tutor because we are not chancing enrolling her in school. She's gonna start going back to NA meetings, and we're going to look into getting her a new addiction specialist. River can have her choice if she wants to go back to school or work with that tutor too. And we're going to get the kid a dog because that is what families do. And, after we do all that—well, maybe before the ring and baby—I'm going to get a job. You're going to finish school. And then, one breath at a time, I'm going to figure out how to give you the moon the way I promised River I would."

Her face got tight, but in the way that told me she was blinking tears back. "You promised River you'd give me the moon?"

I gave her a squeeze, pulling her in, and touched my lips with hers. "Yep. She said her dad already gave you the stars. I can't let him show me up, Cora."

She smiled, those tears breaking free. "And what do I get to give you?"

I stared down into her sparkling, blue eyes, my chest so full that it was almost painful in the most incredible way possible, and I told her the truth. "A reason to breathe.

One in. One out, Cora. Nic may have put those words on your ceiling, but I'm gonna be the man to make sure those breaths come easy and often for all of us. From here on out. All you gotta do is…" I dipped low for another lip touch and whispered, "Breathe."

EPILOGUE

Cora

Ten years later...

"Oh my God, is it broken?" Savannah cried.

"Relax, it's not broken. It's just stuck."

And maybe broken. But, since we were approximately twenty minutes before her wedding was supposed to start and we couldn't get the zipper on her dress up, I spared my eardrums the pain of her shriek and kept that information to myself.

"Move. Let me try," River said, squeezing in front of me. She was wearing a long, purple maid-of-honor gown she hated with a passion. That, I suspected, was the reason Savannah had picked it out in the first place.

After we'd moved to Seattle, Penn had followed through on slipping a ring on my finger. First, a freaking rock of an engagement ring. And then, three months later, at a quiet ceremony in our giant, picturesque backyard, he slipped another ring on and made me Cora Pennington.

A few days later, when I'd gone to the DMV to get a new driver's license, I'd burst into tears at seeing something other than Guerrero as my name. I'd loved Nic, but Penn was right.

He'd left his diamond in a junkyard. And I had been stuck there every day, waiting for someone to find me. I'd fought and struggled to stay at the top of the heap. But, if it hadn't been for Penn, I'm not sure I would have lived long enough to get out.

One day, they would have caught me stealing the money. One day, Marcos's backhand would have landed wrong. One day, Dante wouldn't have stopped.

And, one day, I'd have died, leaving my diamonds— River and Savannah—in that junkyard too.

Instead, I'd found a gorgeous man who loved me and my girls unconditionally and gave me a last name I could feel proud of. And then, two years later, he gave our daughter, Hope, his last name too.

I'd once said nothing had disappointed me, broken me, or destroyed me quite like hope. But that was before I married Penn. Hope no longer felt like the impossible. It felt like the future, and that's exactly what that little girl gave us all. She was eight now, and she had my blue eyes, her father's brown hair, and *all* of River's attitude. She also had a pretty pink bedroom, a warm bed, and not a single lock on her bedroom door.

"Mom," River called, fighting with the zipper. "Can you get me some tweezers? Maybe I can use those to tug it up."

I hurried to my mother-of-the-bride emergency kit and found three different pairs—you know, just in case. Then I carried them all back to her.

For the first few years before Hope was born, River seamlessly alternated between calling me Cora and Mom. There was no rhyme or reason for what she called me or when. It wasn't like she had to hide it anymore. But as soon as Hope was old enough to talk, I was never Cora again. And it wasn't until then that I realized how much I'd missed by letting her call me Cora for all those years. But no more. I was mom. Just mom.

There was a pop before Savannah's dress sagged.

"Oh my God, what was that?" she yelled

"Oh, shit," River breathed, lifting the metal zipper tab hanging off the end of the tweezers.

"What did you do!" Savannah yelled.

While my girls still fought like cats and dogs and loved like sisters, they were all grown up now.

River was twenty-three, taking the slow path through college, living in an apartment across town, and majoring in graphic design. She'd yet to bring a boyfriend home, but she made no secret of leaving her birth control on the bathroom counter so I knew they existed. This could be because she'd learned from Savannah's mistakes and gained a healthy respect for Penn's twitching forehead vein.

Savannah had met a guy her first year at the University of Washington. He seemed nice enough to me, but Penn wanted to string him up by his grungy jeans and long, unwashed hair. Luckily, that guy ended up screwing her over. Obviously, that was not the lucky part. Through heartbreak, she buckled down and focused on her schoolwork, and she ended up falling in love with her professor's dashing teaching assistant, Matthew Lintz. I mean, I couldn't blame her. He was a handsome kid. The problem was that he wasn't really a kid—he was a twenty-two-year-old pre-med student heading off to dental school in the fall. Which, hey, good for him.

They were both in college, so I was fine with it. Penn, however, wanted to string him up by his khaki slacks and preppy crew cut.

In the semi-end, the professor found out. Matthew almost got kicked out and ended up switching schools the last semester before he graduated.

In the real end, we were standing in a church, the zipper on Savannah's dress halfway up, stuck, and now officially broken. All of this happening twenty minutes before her wedding to aforementioned Dr. Matthew Lintz, DMD.

Seriously, the kid could not do *anything* without drama.

"Oh my God. Oh my God. Oh my God," Savannah cried.

"I told you you should have gotten the one with the corset back," River taunted.

Oh! And Savannah was pregnant. This news came a year after the engagement and only three weeks before the wedding, hence the only reason Dr. Matthew Lintz, DMD, was still alive and not buried in my backyard while Penn's muddy boots sat on my back deck.

"Okay, simmer down. I've got this. It's no big deal." I did *not* have it and it was a huge big deal, but I was good in the face of turmoil.

I took the tweezers, shook off the metal tab, and pinched them right onto the head of the zipper. "Okay, suck in for a second."

"I am sucking in!"

River laughed. "Okay, then tell your demon spawn to suck in too."

"Can someone please just go get Dad? He'll know how to fix this."

Savannah had never called Penn anything but dad again. In the beginning, she had done it to tease him. Then, as the months turned into years, she did it to annoy him. But then she started doing it because I think she wanted it to be true. With the way she'd grown up, it was easy to understand why she'd latched onto Penn. And, not surprisingly, Penn had latched right back.

River walked to the door and pulled it open. "Penn, your majesty needs your help."

"She dressed?" he asked cautiously.

"That's uh…kinda what she needs help with. But yeah, she's not naked. Come in."

It had been over a decade since he first walked through the door to my apartment, but I still got chills when he entered a room—the smoking-hot gray suit he was wearing didn't hurt, either.

We were different people now. And Penn wasn't wrong. Different was not bad.

Penn had gone back to investing in real estate, dabbling with a few new builds along the way. And I'd graduated from college and started working as his bookkeeper. I went on maternity leave when I had Hope, and then four years later, I quit altogether when Shane was born. That aptly named little boy looked just like his father. Not even kidding, the child came out scowling. Where Hope had always been a chatter box even before she'd had words, Shane was quiet and stoic, always observing the world around him.

"Hey, baby, what's going—oh, wow." His eyes got wide as he slid his gaze down her strapless, white wedding dress. It was so tasteful and classic that not even over-protective Penn could find something to complain about.

I had never seen Penn cry. Overwhelmed with emotion, absolutely. He'd done the laughing-and-smiling-so-big-your-eyes-start-to-water thing the days Hope and Shane were born. But Savannah was different for him. She had never been a baby, but she was his first daughter to wear a wedding dress.

"Jesus," he breathed, scrubbing a hand over his cheek. "You look beautiful."

She crumbled as he pulled her into a hug. "My dress is broken."

"No crying. Your makeup will run!" I told her as I took off to get a tissue.

When I got back, Penn was already at the back of her dress. "Oh, it's fine. It's not broken. I got this." He reached into his pocket and pulled out some kind multipurpose tool. "I need a hair pin, a mint, and a hockey ticket."

"I'm sorry. What?"

"It was a joke, Cor." He waved me off as he bent to pick up the broken piece of the zipper off the floor. He pinched it back onto the dress, gave it a hard jerk, and zipped it the rest of the way up like it was the easiest thing in the world. Dads were good like that.

"Oh, thank God," Savannah breathed, patting over her heart. She turned, placed a peck on Penn's cheek, and then took off to the bathroom, calling out to River, "I have to pee! It's your duty to hold my dress."

River groaned. "You've been in the dress ten seconds. Why didn't you pee first? I'm not holding your freaking dress." But she said it while walking after her and would no doubt hold her freaking dress.

My husband stole my attention with his lips at my neck. "I'm not sure the mother of the bride is supposed to be this hot."

I laughed. "I'm not sure the mother of the bride is supposed to be thirty-nine and a soon-to-be grandmother, either."

His hands found my hips and he pulled me against his front. "Don't remind me she's having a baby if you want me to get through this ceremony without castrating Matthew."

I grinned, Penn's warmth encompassing me. "Truth or lie."

"Truth," he whispered, leaning down to rest his forehead to mine.

"Truth: You did this. Her being here. Happy. Healthy. Getting married to a good man, who I really believe will be *almost* as good of a dad as she is a mom. You did this, Penn. I love you for a lot of reasons. But today, seeing her—I love you especially for that."

His eyes gentled. "Baby, *you* did this. Me, you, Savannah, River, Hope, Shane. We all have a good life because you never gave up fighting for *yours*."

My nose started to sting, so I reached up and caught the moon necklace he'd wrapped around my neck the day we arrived in Seattle. River wore my star now—not because Penn had asked me to take it off, but because that was the moment I realized I'd lied to Nic when I'd told him that I only wanted him and the stars.

All I'd ever wanted was the moon.

Penn was still as gorgeous as the day I'd met him.

His powerful presence still cast his shadow far and wide.

His skin was still tan, and his short, brown hair was still rich with natural flecks of mahogany and chestnut as though he worked in the sun.

He still had the nose of a Roman gladiator, distinguished and slightly crooked from battle.

His jaw was still composed of sharp, regal angles masked by a thick layer of scruff.

And intricate, black tattoos still traveled down his arms to the backs of his hands.

But there was one thing that had changed about him.

Penn's eyes were no longer a heavy blue—deep and hollow.

Now, Penn's eyes were actually the color of freedom.

For both of us.

I pushed up onto my toes and pressed a kiss to his lips. "Truth: I love you, Penn."

"Truth: I'll always love you, Cora."

THE END

Coming in 2019

THE WAYS WE LIED

Drew and Catalina's story.

OTHER BOOKS

THE RETRIEVAL DUET
Retrieval
Transfer

GUARDIAN PROTECTION AGENCY
Singe
Thrive

THE FALL UP SERIES
The Fall Up
The Spiral Down

THE DARKEST SUNRISE DUET
The Darkest Sunrise
The Brightest Sunset

THE TRUTH DUET
The Truth About Lies
The Truth About Us

THE WRECKED AND RUINED SERIES
Changing Course
Stolen Course
Broken Course
Among the Echoes

ON THE ROPES
Fighting Silence
Fighting Shadows
Fighting Solutude

Savor Me

ABOUT THE AUTHOR

Originally from Savannah, Georgia, *USA Today* bestselling author Aly Martinez now lives in South Carolina with her husband and four young children.

Never one to take herself too seriously, she enjoys cheap wine, mystery leggings, and baked feta. It should be known, however, that she hates pizza and ice cream, almost as much as writing her bio in the third person.

She passes what little free time she has reading anything and everything she can get her hands on, preferably with a super-sized tumbler of wine by her side.

Facebook: www.facebook.com/AuthorAlyMartinez

Facebook Group: www.facebook.com/groups/TheWinery

Twitter: twitter.com/AlyMartinezAuth

Goodreads: www.goodreads.com/AlyMartinez

www.alymartinez.com